THE TIPSY ROBOT

Speedy hopped to a halt and remained standing for a moment—with just a tiny, unsteady weave, as though he were swaying in a light wind.

Powell yelled: "All right, Speedy. Come here, boy."

Whereupon Speedy's robot voice sounded in Powell's earphones for the first time.

It said: "Hot dog, let's play games. You catch me and I'll catch you; no love can cut our knife in two. For I'm Little Buttercup, sweet Little Buttercup. Whoops!" Turning on his heel, he sped off in the direction from which he had come, with a speed and fury that kicked up gouts of baked dust.

And his last words as he receded into the distance were, "There grew a little flower 'neath a great oak tree," followed by a curious metallic clicking that *might* have been the robotic equivalent of a hiccup.

Donovan said weakly: "Where did he pick up the Gilbert and Sullivan? Say, Greg, he . . . he's drunk or something."

—from "Runaround"

THE ASIMOV CHRONICLES

FIFTY YEARS OF ISAAC ASIMOV!

V O L U M E   O N E

EDITED BY MARTIN H. GREENBERG

ACE BOOKS, NEW YORK

"Marooned Off Vesta"—Copyright © 1939 by Ziff-Davis Publishing Co.; renewed © 1967 by Isaac Asimov.

"Robbie" (as "Strange Playfellow")—Copyright © 1940 by Fictioneers, Inc.; renewed © 1967 by Isaac Asimov.

"Nightfall"—Copyright © 1941 by Street & Smith Publications, Inc.; renewed © 1968 by Isaac Asimov.

"Runaround"—Copyright © 1942 by Street & Smith Publications, Inc.; renewed © 1970 by Isaac Asimov.

"Death Sentence"—Copyright © 1943 by Street & Smith Publications, Inc.; renewed © 1971 by Isaac Asimov.

"Catch That Rabbit"—Copyright © 1944 by Street & Smith Publications, Inc.; renewed © 1972 by Isaac Asimov.

"Blind Alley"—Copyright © 1945 by Street & Smith Publications, Inc.; renewed © 1973 by Isaac Asimov.

THE ASIMOV CHRONICLES
VOLUME ONE

An Ace Book / published by arrangement with
Dark Harvest

PRINTING HISTORY
Dark Harvest edition published 1989
Ace edition / August 1990

All rights reserved.
Copyright © 1989 by Nightfall, Inc.
Cover art by Bob Eggleton.
Cover photograph copyright © 1990 by Ben Asen.
This book may not be reproduced in whole or in part,
by mimeograph or any other means, without permission.
For information address: Dark Harvest,
P.O. Box 941, Arlington Heights, Illinois 60006.

ISBN: 0-441-00011-8

Ace Books are published by The Berkley Publishing Group,
200 Madison Avenue, New York, New York 10016.
The name "ACE" and the "A" logo
are trademarks belonging to Charter Communications, Inc.

PRINTED IN THE UNITED STATES OF AMERICA

10 9 8 7 6 5 4 3 2 1

CONTENTS

MAROONED OFF VESTA   1
ROBBIE   21
NIGHTFALL   45
RUNAROUND   87
DEATH SENTENCE   109
CATCH THAT RABBIT   131
BLIND ALLEY   155

THE ASIMOV CHRONICLES

MAROONED OFF VESTA

"Will you please stop walking up and down like that?" said Warren Moore from the couch. "It won't do any of us any good. Think of our blessings; we're airtight, aren't we?"

Mark Brandon whirled and ground his teeth at him. "I'm glad you feel happy about that," he spat out viciously. "Of course, you don't know that our air supply will last only three days." He resumed his interrupted stride with a defiant air.

Moore yawned and stretched, assumed a more comfortable position, and replied, "Expending all that energy will only use it up faster. Why don't you take a hint from Mike here? He's taking it easy."

"Mike" was Michael Shea, late a member of the crew of the *Silver Queen*. His short, squat body was resting on the only chair in the room and his feet were on the only table. He looked up as his name was mentioned, his mouth widening in a twisted grin.

"You've got to expect things like this to happen sometimes," he said. "Bucking the asteroids is risky business. We should've taken the hop. It takes longer, but it's the only safe way. But no, the captain wanted to make the schedule; he *would* go through"—Mike spat disgustedly—"and here we are."

"What's the 'hop'?" asked Brandon.

"Oh, I take it that friend Mike means that we should have

avoided the asteroid belt by plotting a course outside the plane of the ecliptic," answered Moore. "That's it, isn't it, Mike?"

Mike hesitated and then replied cautiously, "Yeah—I guess that's it."

Moore smiled blandly and continued, "Well, I wouldn't blame Captain Crane too much. The repulsion screen must have failed five minutes before that chunk of granite barged into us. That's not his fault, though of course we ought to have steered clear instead of relying on the screen." He shook his head meditatively. "The *Silver Queen* just went to pieces. It's really miraculously lucky that this part of the ship remained intact, and what's more, airtight."

"You've got a funny idea of luck, Warren," said Brandon. "Always have, for as long as I've known you. Here we are in a tenth part of a spaceship, comprising only three *whole* rooms, with air for three days, and no prospect of being alive after that, and you have the infernal gall to prate about luck."

"Compared to the others who died instantly when the asteroid struck, yes," was Moore's answer.

"You think so, eh? Well, let me tell you that instant death isn't so bad compared with what we're going to have to go through. Suffocation is a damned unpleasant way of dying."

"We may find a way out," Moore suggested hopefully.

"Why not face facts!" Brandon's face was flushed and his voice trembled. "We're done, I tell you! Through!"

Mike glanced from one to the other doubtfully and then coughed to attract their attention. "Well, gents, seeing that we're all in the same fix, I guess there's no use hogging things." He drew a small bottle out of his pocket that was filled with a greenish liquid. "Grade A Jabra this is. I ain't too proud to share and share alike."

Brandon exhibited the first signs of pleasure for over a day. "Martian Jabra water. Why didn't you say so before?"

But as he reached for it, a firm hand clamped down upon

his wrist. He looked up into the calm blue eyes of Warren Moore.

"Don't be a fool," said Moore, "there isn't enough to keep us drunk for three days. What do you want to do? Go on a tear now and then die cold sober? Let's save this for the last six hours when the air gets stuffy and breathing hurts—then we'll finish the bottle among us and never *know* when the end comes, or *care*."

Brandon's hand fell away reluctantly. "Damn it, Warren, you'd bleed ice if you were cut. How can you think straight at a time like this?" He motioned to Mike and the bottle was once more stowed away. Brandon walked to the porthole and gazed out.

Moore approached and placed a kindly arm over the shoulders of the younger man. "Why take it so hard, man?" he asked. "You can't last at this rate. Inside of twenty-four hours you'll be a madman if you keep this up."

There was no answer. Brandon stared bitterly at the globe that filled almost the entire porthole, so Moore continued, "Watching Vesta won't do you any good either."

Mike Shea lumbered up to the porthole. "We'd be safe if we were only down there on Vesta. There're people there. How far away are we?"

"Not more than three or four hundred miles judging from its apparent size," answered Moore. "You must remember that it is only two hundred miles in diameter."

"Three hundred miles from salvation," murmured Brandon, "and we might as well be a million. If there were only a way to get ourselves out of the orbit this rotten fragment adopted. You know, manage to give ourselves a push so as to start falling. There'd be no danger of crashing if we did, because that midget hasn't got enough gravity to crush a cream puff."

"It has enough to keep us in the orbit," retorted Brandon. "It must have picked us up while we were lying unconscious after the crash. Wish it had come closer; we might have been able to land on it."

"Funny place, Vesta," observed Mike Shea. "I was down there two-three times. What a dump! It's all covered with some stuff like snow, only it ain't snow. I forget what they call it."

"Frozen carbon dioxide?" prompted Moore.

"Yeah, dry ice, that carbon stuff, that's it. They say that's what makes Vesta so shiny."

"Of course! That would give it a high albedo."

Mike cocked a suspicious eye at Moore and decided to let it pass. "It's hard to see anything down there on account of the snow, but if you look close"—he pointed—"you can see a sort of gray smudge. It think that's Bennett's dome. That's where they keep the observatory. And there is Calorn's dome up there. That's a fuel station, that is. There's plenty more, too, only I don't see them."

He hesitated and then turned to Moore. "Listen, boss, I've been thinking. Wouldn't they be looking for us as soon as they hear about the crash? And wouldn't we be easy to find from Vesta, seeing we're so close?"

Moore shook his head, "No, Mike, they won't be looking for us. No one's going to find out about the crash until the *Silver Queen* fails to turn up on schedule. You see, when the asteroid hit, we didn't have time to send out an SOS"—he sighed—"and they won't find us down there at Vesta, either. We're so small that even at our distance they couldn't see us unless they knew what they were looking for, and exactly where to look."

"Hmm." Mike's forehead was corrugated in deep thought. "Then we've got to get to Vesta before three days are up."

"You've got the gist of the matter, Mike. Now, if we only knew how to go about it, eh?"

Brandon suddenly exploded, "Will you two stop this infernal chitter-chatter and do something? For God's sake, do something."

Moore shrugged his shoulders and without answer returned to the couch. He lounged at ease, apparently carefree, but there was the tiniest crease between his eyes which bespoke concentration.

There was no doubt about it; they *were* in a bad spot. He reviewed the events of the preceding day for perhaps the twentieth time.

After the asteroid had struck, tearing the ship apart, he'd gone out like a light; for how long he didn't know, his own watch being broken and no other timepiece available. When he came to, he found himself, along with Mark Brandon, who shared his room, and Mike Shea, a member of the crew, sole occupants of all that was left of the *Silver Queen*.

This remnant was now careening in an orbit about Vesta. At present things were fairly comfortable. There was a food supply that would last a week. Likewise there was a regional Gravitator under the room that kept them at normal weight and would continue to do so for an indefinite time, certainly for longer than the air would last. The lighting system was less satisfactory but had held on so far.

There was no doubt, however, where the joker in the pack lay. Three days' air! Not that there weren't other disheartening features. There was no heating system— though it would take a long time for the ship to radiate enough heat into the vacuum of space to render them too uncomfortable. Far more important was the fact that their part of the ship had neither a means of communication nor a propulsive mechanism. Moore sighed. One fuel jet in working order would fix everything, for one blast in the right direction would send them safely to Vesta.

The crease between his eyes deepened. What was to be done? They had but one spacesuit among them, one heat ray, and one detonator. That was the sum total of space appliances after a thorough search of the accessible parts of the ship. A pretty hopeless mess, that.

Moore shrugged, rose, and drew himself a glass of water. He swallowed it mechanically, still deep in thought, when an idea struck him. He glanced curiously at the empty cup in his hand.

"Say, Mike," he said, "what kind of water supply have we? Funny that I never thought of that before."

Mike's eyes opened to their fullest extent in an expression of ludicrous surprise. "Didn't you know, boss?"

"Know *what*?" asked Moore impatiently.

"We've got all the water there was." He waved his hand in an all-inclusive gesture. He paused, but as Moore's expression showed nothing but total mystification, he elaborated, "Don't you see? We've got the main tank, the place where all the water for the whole ship was stored." He pointed to one of the walls.

"Do you mean to say that there's a tank full of water adjoining us?"

Mike nodded vigorously, "Yep! Cubic vat a hundred feet each way. And she's three-quarters full."

Moore was astonished. "Seven hundred and fifty thousand cubic feet of water." Then suddenly: "Why hasn't it run out through the broken pipes?"

"It only has one main outlet, which runs down the corridor just outside this room. I was fixing that main when the asteroid hit and had to shut it off. After I came to I opened the pipe leading to our faucet, but that's the only outlet open now."

"Oh." Moore had a curious feeling way down deep inside. An idea had half-formed in his brain, but for the life of him he could not drag it into the light of day. He knew only that there was something in what he had just heard that had some important meaning but he just could not place his finger on it.

Brandon, meanwhile, had been listening to Shea in silence, and now he emitted a short, humorless laugh. "Fate seems to be having its fill of fun with us, I see. First, it puts us within arm's reach of a place of safety and then sees to it that we have no way of getting there.

"Then she provides us with a week's food, three days' air, and *a year's supply of water*. A year's supply, do you hear me? Enough water to drink and to gargle and to wash and to take baths in and—and to do anything else we want. Water—damn the water!"

"Oh, take a less serious view, Mark," said Moore in an attempt to break the younger man's melancholy. "Pretend we're a satellite of Vesta—which we are. We have our own period of revolution and of rotation. We have an equator and an axis. Our 'north pole' is located somewhere toward the top of the porthole, pointing toward Vesta, and our 'south' sticks out away from Vesta through the water tank somewhere. Well, as a satellite, we have an atmosphere, and now, you see, we have a newly discovered ocean.

"And seriously, we're not so badly off. For the three days our atmosphere will last, we can eat double rations and drink ourselves soggy. Hell, we have water enough to throw away—"

The idea which had been half-formed before suddenly sprang to maturity and was nailed. The careless gesture with which he had accompanied the last remark was frozen in mid-air. His mouth closed with a snap and his head came up with a jerk.

But Brandon, immersed in his own thoughts, noticed nothing of Moore's strange actions. "Why don't you complete the analogy to a satellite," he sneered, "or do you, as a Professional Optimist, ignore any and all disagreeable facts? If I were you, I'd continue this way." Here he imitated Moore's voice: "The satellite is at present habitable and inhabited but, due to the approaching depletion of its atmosphere in three days, is expected to become a dead world.

"Well, why don't you answer? Why do you persist in making a joke out of this? Can't you see—*What's the matter?*"

The last was a surprised exclamation and certainly Moore's actions did merit surprise. He had risen suddenly and, after giving himself a smart rap on the forehead, remained stiff and silent, staring into the far distance with gradually narrowing eyelids. Brandon and Mike Shea watched him in speechless astonishment.

Suddenly Moore burst out, "Ha! I've got it. Why didn't I think of it before?" His exclamation degenerated into the unintelligible.

Mike drew out the Jabra bottle with a significant look, but Moore waved it away impatiently. Whereupon Brandon, without any warning, lashed out with his right, catching the surprised Moore flush on the jaw and toppling him.

Moore groaned and rubbed his chin. Somewhat indignant, he asked, "What was the reason for that?"

"Stand up and I'll do it again," shouted Brandon, "I can't stand it anymore. I'm sick and tired of being preached at, and having to listen to your Pollyanna talk. *You're* the one that's going daffy."

"Daffy, nothing! Just a little overexcited, that's all. Listen, for God's sake. I think I know a way—"

Brandon glared at him balefully. "Oh, you do, do you? Raise our hopes with some silly scheme and then find it doesn't work. I won't take it, do you hear? I'll find a real use for the water—drown you—and save some of the air besides."

Moore lost his temper. "Listen, Mark, you're out of this. I'm going through alone. I don't need your help and I don't want it. If you're that sure of dying and that afraid, why not have the agony over? We've got one heat ray and one detonator, both reliable weapons. Take your choice and kill yourself. Shea and I won't interfere." Brandon's lips curled in a last weak gesture of defiance and then suddenly he capitulated, completely and abjectly. "All right, Warren, I'm with you. I—I guess I didn't quite know what I was doing. I don't feel well, Warren. I—I—"

"Aw, that's all right, boy." Moore was genuinely sorry for him. "Take it easy. I know how you feel. It's got me too. But you mustn't give in to it. Fight it, or you'll go stark, raving mad. Now you just try and get some sleep and leave everything to me. Things will turn out right yet."

Brandon, pressing a hand to an aching forehead, stumbled to the couch and tumbled down. Silent sobs shook his frame while Moore and Shea remained in embarrassed silence nearby.

At last Moore nudged Mike. "Come on," he whispered, "let's get busy. We're going places. Airlock five is at the end of the corridor, isn't it?" Shea nodded and Moore continued, "Is it airtight?"

"Well," said Shea after some thought, "the inner door is, of course, but I don't know anything about the outer one. For all I know it may be a sieve. You see, when I tested the wall for airtightness, I didn't dare open the inner door, because if there was anything wrong with the outer one— blooey!" The accompanying gesture was very expressive.

"Then it's up to us to find out about that outer door right now. I've got to get outside some way and we'll just have to take chances. Where's the spacesuit?"

He grabbed the lone suit from its place in the cupboard, threw it over his shoulder and led the way into the long corridor that ran down the side of the room. He passed closed doors behind whose airtight barriers were what once had been passenger quarters but which were now merely cavities, open to space. At the end of the corridor was the tight-fitting door of Airlock 5.

Moore stopped and surveyed it appraisingly. "Looks all right," he observed, "but of course you can't tell what's outside. God, I hope it'll work." He frowned. "Of course we could use the entire corridor as an airlock, with the door to our room as the inner door and this as the outer door, but that would mean the loss of half our air supply. We can't afford that—yet."

He turned to Shea. "All right, now. The indicator shows that the lock was last used for entrance, so it should be full of air. Open the door the tiniest crack, and if there's a hissing noise, shut it quick."

"Here goes," and the lever moved one notch. The mechanism had been severely shaken up during the shock of the crash and its former noiseless workings had given way to a harsh, rasping sound, but it was still in commission. A thin black line appeared on the left-hand side of the lock, marking where the door had slid a fraction of an inch on the runners.

There was no hiss! Moore's look of anxiety faded somewhat. He took a small pasteboard from his pocket and held it against the crack. If air were leaking, that card should have held there, pushed by the escaping gas. It fell to the floor.

Mike Shea stuck a forefinger in his mouth and then put it against the crack. "Thank the Lord," he breathed, "not a sign of a draft."

"Good, good. Open it wider. Go ahead."

Another notch and the crack opened farther. And still no draft. Slowly, ever so slowly, notch by notch, it creaked its way wider and wider. The two men held their breaths, afraid that while not actually punctured, the outer door might have been so weakened as to give way any moment. But it held! Moore was jubilant as he wormed into the spacesuit.

"Things are going fine so far, Mike," he said. "You sit down right here and wait for me. I don't know how long I'll take, but I'll be back. Where's the heat ray? Have you got it?"

Shea held out the ray and asked, "But what are you going to do? I'd sort of like to know."

Moore paused as he was about to buckle on the helmet. "Did you hear me say inside that we had water enough to throw away? Well, I've been thinking it over and that's not such a bad idea. I'm going to throw it away." With no other explanation, he stepped into the lock, leaving behind him a very puzzled Mike Shea.

• • •

It was with a pounding heart that Moore waited for the outer door to open. His plan was an extraordinarily simple one, but it might not be easy to carry out.

There was a sound of creaking gears and scraping ratchets. Air sighed away to nothingness. The door before him slid open a few inches and stuck. Moore's heart sank as for a moment he thought it would not open at all, but after a few preliminary jerks and rattles the barrier slid the rest of the way.

He clicked on the magnetic grapple and very cautiously put a foot out into space. Clumsily he groped his way out to the side of the ship. He had never been outside a ship in open space before and a vast dread overtook him as he clung there, flylike, to his precarious perch. For a moment dizziness overcame him.

He closed his eyes and for five minutes hung there, clutching the smooth sides of what had once been the *Silver Queen*. The magnetic grapple held him firm and when he opened his eyes once more he found his self-confidence in a measure returned.

He gazed about him. For the first time since the crash he saw the stars instead of the vision of Vesta which their porthole afforded. Eagerly he searched the skies for the little blue-white speck that was Earth. It had often amused him that Earth should always be the first object sought by space travelers when stargazing, but the humor of the situation did not strike him now. However, his search was in vain. From where he lay, Earth was invisible. It, as well as the Sun, must be hidden behind Vesta.

Still, there was much else that he could not help but note. Jupiter was off to the left, a brilliant globe the size of a small pea to the naked eye. Moore observed two of its attendant satellites. Saturn was visible too, as a brilliant planet of some negative magnitude, rivaling Venus as seen from Earth.

Moore had expected that a goodly number of asteroids

would be visible—marooned as they were in the asteroid belt—but space seemed surprisingly empty. Once he thought he could see a hurtling body pass within a few miles, but so fast had the impression come and gone that he could not swear that it was not fancy.

And then, of course, there was Vesta. Almost directly below him it loomed like a balloon filling a quarter of the sky. It floated steadily, snowy white, and Moore gazed at it with earnest longing. A good hard kick against the side of the ship, he thought, might start him falling toward Vesta. He *might* land safely and get help for the others. But the chance was too great that he would merely take on a new orbit about Vesta. No, it would have to be better than that.

This reminded him that he had no time to lose. He scanned the side of the ship, looking for the water tank, but all he could see was a jungle of jutting walls, jagged, crumbling, and pointed. He hesitated. Evidently the only thing to do was to make for the lighted porthole to their room and proceed to the tank from there.

Carefully he dragged himself along the wall of the ship. Not five yards from the lock the smoothness stopped abruptly. There was a yawning cavity which Moore recognized as having once been the room adjoining the corridor at the far end. He shuddered. Suppose he were to come across a bloated dead body in one of those rooms. He had known most of the passengers, many of them personally. But he overcame his squeamishness and forced himself to continue his precarious journey toward his goal.

And here he encountered his first practical difficulty. The room itself was made of non-ferrous material in many parts. The magnetic grapple was intended for use only on outer hulls and was useless throughout much of the ship's interior. Moore had forgotten this when suddenly he found himself floating down an incline, his grapple out of use. He grasped and clutched at a nearby projection. Slowly he pulled himself back to safety.

He lay for a moment, almost breathless. Theoretically he

should be weightless out here in space—Vesta's influence being negligible—but the regional Gravitator under his room was working. Without the balance of the other Gravitators, it tended to place him under variable and suddenly shifting stresses as he kept changing his position. For his magnetic grapple to let go suddenly might mean being jerked away from the ship altogether. And then what?

Evidently this was going to be even more difficult than he had thought.

He inched forward in a crawl, testing each spot to see if the grapple would hold. Sometimes he had to make long, circuitous journeys to gain a few feet's headway and at other times he was forced to scramble and slip across small patches of non-ferrous material. And always there was that tiring pull of the Gravitator, continually changing directions as he progressed, setting horizontal floors and vertical walls at queer and almost haphazard angles.

Carefully he investigated all objects that he came across. But it was a barren search. Loose articles, chairs, tables had been jerked away at the first shock, probably, and now were independent bodies of the Solar System. He did manage, however, to pick up a small field glass and fountain pen. These he placed in his pocket. They were valueless under present conditions, but somehow they seemed to make more real this macabre trip across the sides of a dead ship.

For fifteen minutes, twenty, half an hour, he labored slowly toward where he thought the porthole should be. Sweat poured down into his eyes and rendered his hair a matted mass. His muscles were beginning to ache under the unaccustomed strain. His mind, already strained by the ordeal of the previous day, was beginning to waver, to play him tricks.

The crawl began to seem eternal, something that had always existed and would exist forever. The object of the journey, that for which he was striving, seemed unimportant; he only knew that it was necessary to move. The time, one hour back, when he had been with Brandon and Shea, seemed hazy and lost in the far past. That more normal time, two days' age, wholly forgotten.

Only the jagged walls before him, only the vital necessity of getting at some uncertain destination existed in his spinning brain. Grasping, straining, pulling. Feeling for the iron alloy. Up and into gaping holes that were rooms and then out again. Feel and pull—feel and pull—and—a light.

Moore stopped. Had he not been glued to the wall he would have fallen. Somehow that light seemed to clear things. It was the porthole; not the many dark, staring ones he had passed, but alive and alight. Behind it was Brandon. A deep breath and he felt better, his mind cleared.

And now his way lay plain before him. Toward that spark of life he crept. Nearer, and nearer, and nearer until he could touch it. He was there!

His eyes drank in the familiar room. God knows that it hadn't any happy associations in his mind, but it was something real, something almost natural. Brandon slept on the couch. His face was worn and lined but a smile passed over it now and then.

Moore raised his fist to knock. He felt the urgent desire to talk with someone, if only by sign language, yet at the last instant he was refrained. Perhaps the kid was dreaming of home. He was young and sensitive and had suffered much. Let him sleep. Time enough to wake him when—and if—his idea had been carried through.

He located the wall within the room behind which lay the water tank and then tried to spot it from the outside. Now it was not difficult; its rear wall stood out prominently. Moore marveled, for it seemed a miracle that it had escaped puncture. Perhaps the Fates had not been so ironic after all.

Passage to it was easy though it was on the other side of the fragment. What was once a corridor led almost directly to it. Once when the *Silver Queen* had been whole, that corridor had been level and horizontal, but now, under the unbalanced pull of the regional Gravitator, it seemed more of a steep incline than anything else. And yet it made the path simple. Since it was of uniform beryl-steel, Moore found no trouble holding on as he wormed up the twenty-odd feet to the water supply.

And now the crisis—the last stage—had been reached. He felt that he ought to rest first, but his excitement grew rapidly in intensity. It was either now or bust. He pulled himself out to the bottom-center of the tank. There, resting on the small ledge formed by the floor of the corridor that had once extended on that side of the tank, he began operations.

"It's a pity that the main pipe is pointing in the wrong direction," he muttered. "It would have saved me a lot of trouble had it been right. As it is . . ." He sighed and bent to his work. The heat ray was adjusted to maximum concentration and the invisible emanations focused at a spot perhaps a foot above the floor of the tank.

Gradually the effect of the excitatory beam upon the molecules of the wall became noticeable. A spot the size of a dime began shining faintly at the point of focus of the ray gun. It wavered uncertainly, now dimming, now brightening, as Moore strove to steady his tired arm. He propped it on the ledge and achieved better results as the tiny circle of radiation brightened.

Slowly the color ascended the spectrum. The dark, angry red that had first appeared lightened to a cherry color. As the heat continued pouring in, the brightness seemed to ripple out in widening areas, like a target made of successively deepening tints of red. The wall for a distance of some feet from the focal point was becoming uncomfortably hot even though it did not glow and Moore found it necessary to refrain from touching it with the metal of his suit.

Moore cursed steadily, for the ledge itself was also growing hot. It seemed that only imprecations could soothe him. And as the melting wall began to radiate heat in its own right, the chief object of his maledictions were the spacesuit manufacturers. Why didn't they build a suit that could keep heat *out* as well as keep it *in*?

But what Brandon called Professional Optimism crept up. With the salt tang of perspiration in his mouth, he kept consoling himself, "It could be worse, I suppose. At least, the two inches of wall here don't present too much of a barrier. Suppose the tank had been built flush against the outer hull. Whew! Imagine trying to melt through a foot of this." He gritted his teeth and kept on.

The spot of brightness was now flickering into the orange-yellow and Moore knew that the melting point of the beryl-steel alloy would soon be reached. He found himself forced to watch the spot only at widely spaced intervals and then only for fleeting moments.

Evidently it would have to be done quickly if it were to be done at all. The heat ray had not been fully loaded in the first place, and, pouring out energy at maximum as it had been doing for almost ten minutes now, must be approaching exhaustion. Yet the wall was just barely passing the plastic stage. In a fever of impatience, Moore jammed the muzzle of the gun directly at the center of the spot, drawing it back speedily.

A deep depression formed in the soft metal, but a puncture had not been formed. However, Moore was satisfied. He was almost there now. Had there been air between himself and the wall, he would undoubtedly have heard the gurgling and the hissing of the steaming water within. The pressure was building up. How long would the weakened wall endure?

Then so suddenly that Moore did not realize it for a few moments, he was through. A tiny fissure formed at the bottom of that little pit made by the ray gun and in less time than it takes to imagine, the churning water within had its way.

The soft, liquid metal at that spot puffed out, sticking out raggedly around a pea-sized hole. And from that hole there came a hissing and a roaring. A cloud of steam emerged and enveloped Moore.

Through the mist he could see the steam condense almost immediately to ice droplets and saw these icy pellets shrink rapidly into nothingness.

For fifteen minutes he watched the steam shoot out.

Then he became aware of gentle pressure pushing him away from the ship. A savage joy welled up within him as he realized that this was the effect of acceleration on the ship's part. His own inertia was holding him back.

That meant his work had been finished—and successfully. That stream of water was substituting for the rocket blast.

He started back.

If the horrors and dangers of the journey to the tank had been great, those of the way back should have been greater. He was infinitely more tired, his aching eyes were all but blind, and added to the crazy pull of the Gravitator was the force induced by the varying acceleration of the ship. But whatever his labors to return, they did not bother him. In later time, he never even remembered the heartbreaking trip.

How he managed to negotiate the distance in safety he did not know. Most of the time he was lost in a haze of happiness, scarcely realizing the actualities of the situation. His mind was filled with one thought only—to get back quickly, to tell the happy news of their escape.

Suddenly he found himself before the airlock. He hardly grasped the fact that it *was* the airlock. He almost did not understand why he pressed the signal button. Some instinct told him it was the thing to do.

Mike Shea was waiting. There was a creak and a rumble and the outer door started opening, caught, and stopped at the same place as before, but once again it managed to slide the rest of the way. It closed behind Moore, then the inner door opened and he stumbled into Shea's arms.

As in a dream he felt himself half-pulled, half-carried

down the corridor to the room. His suit was ripped off. A hot, burning liquid stung his throat. Moore gagged, swallowed, and felt better. Shea pocketed the Jabra bottle once more.

The blurred, shifting images of Brandon and Shea before him steadied and became solid. Moore wiped the perspiration from his face with a trembling hand and essayed a weak smile.

"Wait," protested Brandon, "don't say anything. You look half-dead. Rest, will you!"

But Moore shook his head. In a hoarse, cracked voice he narrated as well as he could the events of the past two hours. The tale was incoherent, scarcely intelligible but marvelously impressive. The two listeners scarcely breathed during the recital.

"You mean," stammered Brandon, "that the water spout is pushing us toward Vesta, like a rocket exhaust?"

"Exactly—same thing as—rocket exhaust," panted Moore. "Action and reaction. Is located—on side opposite Vesta—hence pushing us toward Vesta."

Shea was dancing before the porthole. "He's right, Brandon, me boy. You can make out Bennett's dome as clear as day. We're getting there, we're getting there."

Moore felt himself recovering. "We're approaching in spiral path on account of original orbit. We'll land in five or six hours probably. The water will last for quite a long while and the pressure is still great, since the water issues as steam."

"Steam—at the low temperature of space?" Brandon was surprised.

"Steam—at the low pressure of space!" corrected Moore. "The boiling point of water falls with the pressure. It is very low indeed in a vacuum. Even ice has a vapor pressure sufficient to sublime."

He smiled. "As a matter of fact, it freezes and boils at the same time. I watched it." A short pause, then, "Well, how do you feel now, Brandon? Much better, eh?"

Brandon reddened and his face fell. He groped vainly for words for a few moments. Finally he said in a half-whisper, "You know, I must have acted like a damn fool and a coward at first. I—I guess I don't deserve all this after going to pieces and letting the burden of our escape rest on your shoulders.

"I wish you'd beat me up, or something, for punching you before. It'd make me feel better. I mean it." And he really did seem to mean it.

Moore gave him an affectionate push. "Forget it. You'll never know how near I came to breaking down myself." He raised his voice in order to drown out any further apologies on Brandon's part, "Hey, Mike, stop staring out of that porthole and bring over that Jabra bottle."

Mike obeyed with alacrity, bringing with him three Plexatron units to be used as makeshift cups. Moore filled each precisely to the brim. He was going to be drunk with a vengeance.

"Gentlemen," he said solemnly, "a toast." The three raised the mugs in unison, "Gentlemen, I give you the year's supply of good old H_2O *we used to have*."

ROBBIE

"Ninety-eight—ninety-nine—*one hundred*." Gloria withdrew her chubby little forearm from before her eyes and stood for a moment, wrinkling her nose and blinking in the sunlight. Then, trying to watch in all directions at once, she withdrew a few cautious steps from the tree against which she had been leaning.

She craned her neck to invesitgate the possibilities of a clump of bushes to the right and then withdrew farther to obtain a better angle for viewing its dark recesses. The quiet was profound except for the incessant buzzing of insects and the occasional chirrup of some hardy bird, braving the midday sun.

Gloria pouted, "I bet he went inside the house, and I've told him a million times that that's not fair."

With tiny lips pressed together tightly and a severe frown crinkling her forehead, she moved determinedly toward the two-story building up past the driveway.

Too late she heard the rustling sound behind her, followed by the distinctive and rhythmic clump-clump of Robbie's metal feet. She whirled about to see her triumphing companion emerge from hiding and make for the home-tree at full speed.

Gloria shrieked in dismay. "Wait, Robbie! That wasn't fair, Robbie! You promised you wouldn't run until I found you." Her little feet could make no headway at all against

Robbie's giant strides. Then, within ten feet of the goal, Robbie's pace slowed suddenly to the merest of crawls, and Gloria, with one final burst of wild speed, dashed pantingly past him to touch the welcome bark of home-tree first.

Gleefully, she turned on the faithful Robbie, and with the basest of ingratitude, rewarded him for his sacrifice, by taunting him cruelly for a lack of running ability.

"Robbie can't run," she shouted at the top of her eight-year-old voice. "I can beat him any day. I can beat him any day." She chanted the words in a shrill rhythm.

Robbie didn't answer, of course—not in words. He pantomimed running, instead, inching away until Gloria found herself running after him as he dodged her narrowly, forcing her to veer in helpless circles, little arms outstretched and fanning at the air.

"Robbie," she squealed, "stand still!" —And the laughter was forced out of her in breathless jerks.

—Until he turned suddenly and caught her up, whirling her round, so that for her the world fell away for a moment with a blue emptiness beneath, and green trees stretching hungrily downward toward the void. Then she was down in the grass again, leaning against Robbie's leg and still holding a hard, metal finger.

After a while, her breath returned. She pushed uselessly at her disheveled hair in vague imitation of one of her mother's gestures and twisted to see if her dress were torn.

She slapped her hand against Robbie's torso, "Bad boy! I'll spank you!"

And Robbie cowered, holding his hands over his face so that she had to add, "No, I won't, Robbie, I won't spank you. But anyway, it's my turn to hide now because you've got longer legs and you promised not to run till I found you."

Robbie nodded his head—a small parallelepiped with rounded edges and corners attached to a similar but much larger parallelepiped that served as torso by means of a short, flexible stalk—and obediently faced the tree. A thin, metal film descended over his glowing eyes and from within his body came a steady, resonant ticking.

"Don't peek now—and don't skip any numbers," warned Gloria, and scurried for cover.

With unvarying regularity, seconds were ticked off, and at the hundredth, up went the eyelids, and the glowing red of Robbie's eyes swept the prospect. They rested for a moment on a bit of colorful gingham that protruded from behind a boulder. He advanced a few steps and convinced himself that it was Gloria who squatted behind it.

Slowly, remaining always between Gloria and home-tree, he advanced on the hiding place, and when Gloria was plainly in sight and could no longer even theorize to herself that she was not seen, he extended one arm toward her, slapping the other against his leg so that it rang again. Gloria emerged sulkily.

"You peeked!" she exclaimed, with gross unfairness. "Besides I'm tired of playing hide-and-seek. I want a ride."

But Robbie was hurt at the unjust accusation, so he seated himself carefully and shook his head ponderously from side to side.

Gloria changed her tone to one of gentle coaxing immediately, "Come on, Robbie. I didn't mean it about the peeking. Give me a ride."

Robbie was not to be won over so easily, though. He gazed stubbornly at the sky, and shook his head even more emphatically.

"Please, Robbie, please give me a ride." She encircled his neck with rosy arms and hugged tightly. Then, changing moods in a moment, she moved away. "If you don't, I'm going to cry," and her face twisted appallingly in preparation.

Hard-hearted Robbie paid scant attention to this dreadful possibility, and shook his head a third time. Gloria found it necessary to play her trump card.

"If you don't," she exclaimed warmly, "I won't tell you any more stories, that's all. Not one—"

Robbie gave in immediately and unconditionally before this ultimatum, nodding his head vigorously until the metal of his neck hummed. Carefully, he raised the little girl and placed her on his broad, flat shoulders.

Gloria's threatened tears vanished immediately and she crowed with delight. Robbie's metal skin, kept at a constant temperature of seventy by the high resistance coils within felt nice and comfortable, while the beautifully loud sound her heels made as they bumped rhythmically against his chest was enchanting.

"You're an air-coaster, Robbie, you're a big, silver air-coaster. Hold out your arms straight. —You *got* to, Robbie, if you're going to be an air-coaster."

The logic was irrefutable. Robbie's arms were wings catching the air currents and he was a silver 'coaster.

Gloria twisted the robot's head and leaned to the right. He banked sharply. Gloria equipped the 'coaster with a motor that went "B-r-r-r" and then with weapons that went "Powie" and "Sh-sh-shshsh." Pirates were giving chase and the ship's blasters were coming into play. The pirates dropped in a steady rain.

"Got another one. —Two more," she cried.

Then "Faster, men," Gloria said pompously, "we're running out of ammunition." She aimed over her shoulder with undaunted courage and Robbie was a blunt-nosed spaceship zooming through the void at maximum acceleration.

Clear across the field he sped, to the patch of tall grass on the other side, where he stopped with a suddenness that evoked a shriek from his flushed rider, and then tumbled her onto the soft, green carpet.

Gloria gasped and panted, and gave voice to intermittent whispered exclamations of "That was *nice!*"

Robbie waited until she had caught her breath and then pulled gently at a lock of hair.

"You want something?" said Gloria, eyes wide in an

apparently artless complexity that fooled her huge "nurse-maid" not at all. He pulled the curl harder.

"Oh, I know. You want a story."

Robbie nodded rapidly.

"Which one?"

Robbie made a semi-circle in the air with one finger.

The little girl protested, "*Again*? I've told you Cinderella a million times. Aren't you tired of it? —It's for babies."

Another semi-circle.

"Oh, well," Gloria composed herself, ran over the details of the tale in her mind (together with her own elaborations, of which she had several) and began:

"Are you ready? Well—once upon a time there was a beautiful little girl whose name was Ella. And she had a terribly cruel step-mother and two very ugly and *very* cruel step-sisters and—"

Gloria was reaching the very climax of the tale—midnight was striking and everything was changing back to the shabby originals lickety-split, while Robbie listened tensely with burning eyes—when the interruption came.

"Gloria!"

It was the high-pitched sound of a woman who has been calling not once, but several times; and had the nervous tone of one in whom anxiety was beginning to overcome impatience.

"Mamma's calling me," said Gloria, not quite happily. "You'd better carry me back to the house, Robbie."

Robbie obeyed with alacrity for somehow there was that in him which judged it best to obey Mrs. Weston, without as much as a scrap of hesitation. Gloria's father was rarely home in the daytime except on Sunday—today, for instance—and when he was, he proved a genial and under-standing person. Gloria's mother, however, was a source of uneasiness to Robbie and there was always the impulse to sneak away from her sight.

Mrs. Weston caught sight of them the minute they rose

above the masking tufts of long grass and retired inside the house to wait.

"I've shouted myself hoarse, Gloria," she said, severely. "Where were you?"

"I was with Robbie," quavered Gloria. "I was telling him Cinderella, and I forgot it was dinner-time."

"Well, it's a pity Robbie forgot, too." Then, as if that reminded her of the robot's presence, she whirled upon him. "You may go, Robbie. She doesn't need you now." Then, brutally, "And don't come back till I call you."

Robbie turned to go, but hesitated as Gloria cried out in his defense, "Wait, Mamma, you got to let him stay. I didn't finish Cinderella for him. I said I would tell him Cinderella and I'm not finished."

"Gloria!"

"Honest and truly, Mamma, he'll stay so quiet, you won't even know he's here. He can sit on the chair in the corner, and he won't say a word,—I mean he won't *do* anything. Will you, Robbie?"

Robbie, appealed to, nodded his massive head up and down once.

"Gloria, if you don't stop this at once, you shan't see Robbie for a whole week."

The girl's eyes fell, "All right! But Cinderella is his favorite story and I didn't finish it. —And he likes it so much."

The robot left with a disconsolate step and Gloria choked back a sob.

George Weston was comfortable. It was a habit of his to be comfortable on Sunday afternoons. A good, hearty dinner below the hatches; a nice, soft, dilapidated couch on which to sprawl; a copy of the *Times*; slippered feet and shirtless chest;—how could anyone *help* but be comfortable?

He wasn't pleased, therefore, when his wife walked in. After ten years of married life, he still was so unutterably foolish as to love her, and there was no question that he was always glad to see her—still Sunday afternoons just after dinner were sacred to him and his idea of solid comfort was to be left in utter solitude for two or three hours. Consequently, he fixed his eyes firmly upon the latest reports of the Lefebre-Yoshida expedition to Mars (this one was to take off from Lunar Base and might actually succeed) and pretended she wasn't there.

Mrs. Weston waited patiently for two minutes, then impatiently for two more, and finally broke the silence.

"George!"

"Hmpph?"

"George, I say! *Will* you put down that paper and look at me?"

The paper rustled to the floor and Weston turned a weary face toward his wife, "What is it, dear?"

"You know what it is, George. It's Gloria and that terrible machine."

"What terrible machine?"

"Now don't you pretend you don't know what I'm talking about. It's that robot Gloria calls Robbie. He doesn't leave her for a moment."

"Well, why should he? He's not supposed to. And he certainly isn't a terrible machine. He's the best darn robot money can buy and I'm damned sure he set me back half a year's income. He's worth it, though—darn sight cleverer than half my office staff."

He made a move to pick up the paper again, but his wife was quicker and snatched it away.

"You listen to *me*, George. I won't have my daughter entrusted to a machine—and I don't care how clever it is. It has no soul, and no one knows what it may be thinking. A child just isn't *made* to be guarded by a thing of metal!"

Weston frowned, "When did you decide this? He's been with Gloria two years now and I haven't seen you worry till now."

"It was different at first. It was a novelty; it took a load off me, and—and it was a fashionable thing to do. But now I don't know. The neighbors—"

"Well, what have the neighbors to do with it? Now, look. A robot is infinitely more to be trusted than a human nursemaid. Robbie was constructed for only one purpose really—to be the companion of a little child. His entire 'mentality' has been created for the purpose. He just can't help being faithful and loving and kind. He's a machine—*made so*. That's more than you can say for humans."

"But something might go wrong. Some—some—" Mrs. Weston was a bit hazy about the insides of a robot, "some little jigger will come loose and the awful thing will go berserk and—and—" She couldn't bring herself to complete the quite obvious thought.

"Nonsense," Weston denied, with an involuntary nervous shiver. "That's completely ridiculous. We had a long discussion at the time we bought Robbie about the First Law of Robotics. You *know* that it is impossible for a robot to harm a human being; that long before enough can go wrong to alter that First Law, a robot would be completely inoperable. It's a mathematical impossibility. Besides, I have an engineer from U.S. Robots here twice a year to give the poor gadget a complete overhaul. Why, there's no more chance of anything at all going wrong with Robbie than there is of you or I suddenly going looney—considerably less, in fact. Besides, how are you going to take him away from Gloria?"

He made another futile stab at the paper and his wife tossed it angrily into the next room.

"That's just it, George! She won't play with anyone else. There are dozens of little boys and girls that she should make friends with, but she won't. She won't go *near* them unless I make her. That's no way for a little girl to grow up. You want her to be normal, don't you? You want her to be able to take her part in society."

"You're jumping at shadows, Grace. Pretend Robbie's a dog. I've seen hundreds of children who would rather have their dog than their father."

"A dog is different, George. We *must* get rid of that horrible thing. You can sell it back to the company. I've asked, and you can."

"You've *asked*? Now look here, Grace, let's not go off the deep end. We're keeping that robot until Gloria is older and I don't want the subject brought up again." And with that he walked out of the room in a huff.

Mrs. Weston met her husband at the door two evenings later. "You'll have to listen to this, George. There's bad feeling in the village."

"About what?" asked Weston. He stepped into the washroom and drowned out any possible answer by the splash of water.

Mrs. Weston waited. She said, "About Robbie."

Weston stepped out, towel in hand, face red and angry, "What are you talking about?"

"Oh, it's been building up. I've tried to close my eyes to it, but I'm not going to any more. Most of the villagers consider Robbie dangerous. Children aren't allowed to go near our place in the evenings."

"We trust *our* child with the thing."

"Well, people aren't reasonable about these things."

"Then to hell with them."

"Saying that doesn't solve the problem. I've got to do my shopping down there. I've got to meet them every day. And it's even worse in the city these days when it comes to robots. New York has just passed an ordinance keeping all robots off the streets between sunset and sunrise."

"All right, but they can't stop us from keeping a robot in our home. —Grace, this is one of your campaigns. I recognize it. But it's no use. The answer is still, no! We're keeping Robbie!"

And yet he loved his wife—and what was worse, his wife knew it. George Weston, after all, was only a man—poor thing—and his wife made full use of every device which a

clumsier and more scrupulous sex had learned, with reason
and futility, to fear.

Ten times in the ensuing week, he cried, "Robbie
stays,—and that's *final*!" and each time it was weaker and
accompanied by a louder and more agonized groan.

Came the day at last, when Weston approached his
daughter guiltily and suggested a "beautiful" visivox show
in the village.

Gloria clapped her hands happily, "Can Robbie go?"

"No, dear," he said, and winced at the sound of his
voice, "they don't allow robots at the visivox—but you can
tell him all about it when you get home." He stumbled all
over the last few words and looked away.

Gloria came back from town bubbling over with enthusiasm, for the visivox had been a gorgeous spectacle
indeed.

She waited for her father to maneuver the jet-car into the
sunken garage. "Wait till I tell Robbie, Daddy. He would
have liked it like anything. —Especially when Francis Fran
was backing away so-o-o quietly, and backed right into one
of the Leopard-Men and had to run." She laughed again,
"Daddy, are there really Leopard-Men on the Moon?"

"Probably not," said Weston absently. "It's just funny
make-believe." He couldn't take much longer with the car.
He'd have to face it.

Gloria ran across the lawn. "Robbie. —Robbie!"

Then she stopped suddenly at the sight of a beautiful
collie which regarded her out of serious brown eyes as it
wagged its tail on the porch.

"Oh, what a nice dog!" Gloria climbed the steps,
approached cautiously and patted it. "Is it for me, Daddy?"

Her mother had joined them. "Yes, it is, Gloria. Isn't it
nice—soft and funny. It's very gentle. It *likes* little girls."

"Can he play games?"

"Surely. He can do any number of tricks. Would you like
to see some?"

"Right away. I want Robbie to see him, too. —*Robbie!*"

She stopped, uncertainly, and frowned, "I'll bet he's just staying in his room because he's mad at me for not taking him to the visivox. You'll have to explain to him, Daddy. He might not believe me, but he knows if you say it, it's so."

Weston's lips grew tighter. He looked toward his wife but could not catch her eye.

Gloria turned precipitously and ran down the basement steps, shouting as she went, "Robbie— Come and see what Daddy and Mamma brought me. They brought me a dog, Robbie."

In a minute she had returned, a frightened little girl. "Mamma, Robbie isn't in his room. Where is he?" There was no answer and George Weston coughed and was suddenly extremely interested in an aimlessly drifting cloud. Gloria's voice quavered on the verge of tears, "Where's Robbie, Mamma?"

Mrs. Weston sat down and drew her daughter gently to her, "Don't feel bad, Gloria. Robbie has gone away, I think."

"Gone *away*? Where? Where's he gone away, Mamma?"

"No one knows, darling. He just walked away. We've looked and we've looked and we've looked for him, but we can't find him."

"You mean he'll never come back again?" Her eyes were round with horror.

"We may find him soon. We'll keep looking for him. And meanwhile you can play with your nice new doggie. Look at him! His name is Lightning and he can—"

But Gloria's eyelids had overflown, "I don't want the nasty dog—I want Robbie. I want you to find me Robbie." Her feelings became too deep for words, and she spluttered into a shrill wail.

Mrs. Weston glanced at her husband for help, but he merely shuffled his feet morosely and did not withdraw his ardent stare from the heavens, so she bent to the task of consolation, "Why do you cry, Gloria? Robbie was only a machine, just a nasty old machine. He wasn't alive at all."

"He was *not* a machine!" screamed Gloria, fiercely and ungrammatically. "He was a *person* just like you and me and he was my *friend*. I want him back. Oh, Mamma, I want him back."

Her mother groaned in defeat and left Gloria to her sorrow.

"Let her have her cry out," she told her husband. "Childish griefs are never lasting. In a few days, she'll forget that awful robot ever existed."

But time proved Mrs. Weston a bit too optimistic. To be sure, Gloria ceased crying, but she ceased smiling, too, and the passing days found her ever more silent and shadowy. Gradually, her attitude of passive unhappiness wore Mrs. Weston down and all that kept her from yielding was the impossibility of admitting defeat to her husband.

Then, one evening, she flounced into the living room, sat down, folded her arms and looked boiling mad.

Her husband stretched his neck in order to see her over his newspaper, "What now, Grace?"

"It's that child, George. I've had to send back the dog today. Gloria positively couldn't stand the sight of him, she said. She's driving me into a nervous breakdown."

Weston laid down the paper and a hopeful gleam entered his eyes, "Maybe— Maybe we ought to get Robbie back. It might be done, you know. I can get in touch with—"

"No!" she replied, grimly. "I won't hear of it. We're not giving up that easily. My child shall *not* be brought up by a robot if it takes years to break her of it."

Weston picked up his paper again with a disappointed air. "A year of this will have me prematurely gray."

"You're a big help, George," was the frigid answer. "What Gloria needs is a change of environment. Of course she can't forget Robbie here. How can she when every tree and rock reminds her of him? It is really the *silliest* situation I have ever heard of. Imagine a child pining away for the loss of a robot."

"Well, stick to the point. What's the change in environment you're planning?"

"We're going to take her to New York."

"The city! In August! Say, do you know what New York is like in August? It's unbearable."

"Millions do bear it."

"They don't have a place like this to go to. If they didn't have to stay in New York, they wouldn't."

"Well, *we* have to. I say we're leaving now—or as soon as we can make the arrangements. In the city, Gloria will find sufficient interests and sufficient friends to perk her up and make her forget that machine."

"Oh, Lord," groaned the lesser half, "those frying pavements!"

"We have to," was the unshaken response. "Gloria has lost five pounds in the last month and my little girl's health is more important to me than your comfort."

"It's a pity you didn't think of your little girl's health before you deprived her of her pet robot," he muttered—but to himself.

Gloria displayed immediate signs of improvement when told of the impending trip to the city. She spoke little of it, but when she did, it was always with lively anticipation. Again, she began to smile and to eat with something of her former appetite.

Mrs. Weston hugged herself for joy and lost no opportunity to triumph over her still skeptical husband.

"You see, George, she helps with the packing like a little angel, and chatters away as if she hadn't a care in the world. It's just as I told you—all we need do is substitute other interests."

"Hmpph," was the skeptical response, "I hope so."

Preliminaries were gone through quickly. Arrangements were made for the preparation of their city home and a couple were engaged as housekeepers for the country home. When the day of the trip finally did come, Gloria was all but her old self again, and no mention of Robbie passed her lips at all.

In high good-humor the family took a taxi-gyro to the airport (Weston would have preferred using his own private 'gyro, but it was only a two-seater with no room for baggage) and entered the waiting liner.

"Come, Gloria," called Mrs. Weston. "I've saved you a seat near the window so you can watch the scenery."

Gloria trotted down the aisle cheerily, flattened her nose into a white oval against the thick clear glass, and watched with an intentness that increased as the sudden coughing of the motor drifted backward into the interior. She was too young to be frightened when the ground dropped away as if let through a trap-door and she herself suddenly became twice her usual weight, but not too young to be mightily interested. It wasn't until the ground had changed into a tiny patch-work quilt that she withdrew her nose, and faced her mother again.

"Will we soon be in the city, Mamma?" she asked, rubbing her chilled nose, and watching with interest as the patch of moisture which her breath had formed on the pane shrank slowly and vanished.

"In about half an hour, dear." Then, with just the faintest trace of anxiety, "Aren't you glad we're going? Don't you think you'll be very happy in the city with all the buildings and people and things to see? We'll go to the visivox every day and see shows and go to the circus and the beach and—"

"Yes, Mamma," was Gloria's unenthusiastic rejoinder. The liner passed over a bank of clouds at the moment, and Gloria was instantly absorbed in the unusual spectacle of clouds underneath one. Then they were over clear sky again, and she turned to her mother with a sudden mysterious air of secret knowledge.

"*I* know why we're going to the city, Mamma."

"Do you?" Mrs. Weston was puzzled. "Why, dear?"

"You didn't tell me because you wanted it to be a

surprise, but *I* know." For a moment, she was lost in admiration at her own acute penetration, and then she laughed gaily. "We're going to New York so we can find Robbie, aren't we? —With detectives."

The statement caught George Weston in the middle of a drink of water, with disastrous results. There was a sort of strangled gasp, a geyser of water, and then a bout of choking coughs. When all was over, he stood there, a red-faced, water-drenched and very, very annoyed person.

Mrs. Weston maintained her composure, but when Gloria repeated her question in a more anxious tone of voice, she found her temper rather bent.

"Maybe," she retorted tartly. "Now sit and be still, for Heaven's sake."

New York City, 1998 A.D., was a paradise for the sight-seer more than ever in its history. Gloria's parents realized this and made the most of it.

On direct orders from his wife, George Weston arranged to have his business take care of itself for a month or so, in order to be free to spend the time in what he termed "dissipating Gloria to the verge of ruin." Like everything else Weston did, this was gone about in an efficient, thorough, and business-like way. Before the month had passed, nothing that could be done had not been done.

She was taken to the top of the half-mile-tall Roosevelt Building, to gaze down in awe upon the jagged panorama of rooftops that blended far off in the fields of Long Island and the flatlands of New Jersey. They visited the zoos where Gloria stared in delicious fright at the "real live lion" (rather disappointed that the keepers fed him raw steaks, instead of human beings, as she had expected), and asked insistently and peremptorily to see "the whale."

The various museums came in for their share of attention, together with the parks and the beaches and the aquarium.

She was taken halfway up the Hudson in an excursion steamer fitted out in the archaism of the mad Twenties. She travelled into the stratosphere on an exhibition trip, where the sky turned deep purple and the stars came out and the misty earth below looked like a huge concave bowl. Down under the waters of the Long Island Sound she was taken in a glass-walled sub-sea vessel, where in a green and wavering world, quaint and curious sea-things ogled her and wiggled suddenly away.

On a more prosaic level, Mrs. Weston took her to the department stores where she could revel in another type of fairyland.

In fact, when the month had nearly sped, the Westons were convinced that everything conceivable had been done to take Gloria's mind once and for all off the departed Robbie—but they were not quite sure they had succeeded.

The fact remained that wherever Gloria went, she displayed the most absorbed and concentrated interest in such robots as happened to be present. No matter how exciting the spectacle before her, nor how novel to her girlish eyes, she turned away instantly if the corner of her eye caught a glimpse of metallic movement.

Mrs. Weston went out of her way to keep Gloria away from all robots.

And the matter was finally climaxed in the episode at the Museum of Science and Industry. The Museum had announced a special "children's program" in which exhibits of scientific witchery scaled down to the child mind were to be shown. The Westons, of course, placed it upon their list of "absolutely."

It was while the Westons were standing totally absorbed in the exploits of a powerful electro-magnet that Mrs. Weston suddenly became aware of the fact that Gloria was no longer with her. Initial panic gave way to calm decision and, enlisting the aid of three attendants, a careful search was begun.

Gloria, of course, was not one to wander aimlessly, however. For her age, she was an unusually determined and purposeful girl, quite full of the maternal genes in that respect. She had seen a huge sign on the third floor, which had said, "This Way to the Talking Robot." Having spelled it out to herself and having noticed that her parents did not seem to wish to move in the proper direction, she did the obvious thing. Waiting for an opportune moment of parental distraction, she calmly disengaged herself and followed the sign.

The Talking Robot was a *tour de force*, a thoroughly impractical device, possessing publicity value only. Once an hour, an escorted group stood before it and asked questions of the robot engineer in charge in careful whispers. Those the engineer decided were suitable for the robot's circuits were transmitted to the Talking Robot.

It was rather dull. It may be nice to know that the square of fourteen is one hundred ninety-six, that the temperature at the moment is 72 degrees Fahrenheit, and the air-pressure 30.02 inches of mercury, that the atomic weight of sodium is 23, but one doesn't really need a robot for that. One especially does not need an unwieldy, totally immobile mass of wires and coils spreading over twenty-five square yards.

Few people bothered to return for a second helping, but one girl in her middle teens sat quietly on a bench waiting for a third. She was the only one in the room when Gloria entered.

Gloria did not look at her. To her at the moment, another human being was but an inconsiderable item. She saved her attention for this large thing with the wheels. For a moment, she hesitated in dismay. It didn't look like any robot she had ever seen.

Cautiously and doubtfully she raised her treble voice, "Please, Mr. Robot, sir, are you the Talking Robot, sir?" She wasn't sure, but it seemed to her that a robot that actually talked was worth a great deal of politeness.

(The girl in her mid-teens allowed a look of intense

concentration to cross her thin, plain face. She whipped out a small notebook and began writing in rapid pot-hooks.)

There was an oily whir of gears and a mechanically-timbered voice boomed out in words that lacked accent and intonation, "I—am—the—robot—that—talks."

Gloria stared at it ruefully. It *did* talk, but the sound came from inside somewheres. There was no *face* to talk to. She said, "Can you help me, Mr. Robot, sir?"

The Talking Robot was designed to answer questions, and only such questions as it could answer had ever been put to it. It was quite confident of its ability, therefore, "I—can—help—you."

"Thank you, Mr. Robot, sir. Have you seen Robbie?"

"Who—is—Robbie?"

"He's a robot, Mr. Robot, sir." She stretched to tip-toes. "He's about so high, Mr. Robot, sir, only higher, and he's very nice. He's got a head, you know. I mean you haven't; but he has, Mr. Robot, sir."

The Talking Robot had been left behind, "A—robot?"

"Yes, Mr. Robot, sir. A robot just like you, except he can't talk, of course, and—looks like a real person."

"A—robot—like—me?"

"Yes, Mr. Robot, sir."

To which the Talking Robot's only response was an erratic splutter and an occasional incoherent sound. The radical generalization offered it, i.e., its existence, not as a particular object, but as a member of a general group, was too much for it. Loyally, it tried to encompass the concept and half a dozen coils burnt out. Little warning signals were buzzing.

(The girl in her mid-teens left at that point. She had enough for her Physics-1 paper on "Practical Aspects of Robotics." This paper was Susan Calvin's first of many on the subject.)

Gloria stood waiting, with carefully concealed impatience, for the machine's answer when she heard the cry behind her of "There she is," and recognized that cry as her mother's.

"What are you doing here, you bad girl?" cried Mrs. Weston, anxiety dissolving at once into anger. "Do you know you frightened your mamma and daddy almost to death? Why did you run away?"

The robot engineer had also dashed in, tearing his hair, and demanding who of the gathering crowd had tampered with the machine. "Can't anybody read signs?" he yelled. "You're not allowed in here without an attendant."

Gloria raised her grieved voice over the din, "I only came to see the Talking Robot, Mamma. I thought he might know where Robbie was because they're both robots." And then, as the thought of Robbie was suddenly brought forcefully home to her, she burst into a sudden storm of tears, "And I *got* to find Robbie, Mamma. I *got* to."

Mrs. Weston strangled a cry, and said, "Oh, good Heavens. Come home, George. This is more than I can stand."

That evening, George Weston left for several hours, and the next morning, he approached his wife with something that looked suspiciously like smug complacence.

"I've got an idea, Grace."

"About what?" was the gloomy, uninterested query.

"About Gloria."

"You're not going to suggest buying back that robot?"

"No, of course not."

"Then go ahead. I might as well listen to you. Nothing *I've* done seems to have done any good."

"All right. Here's what I've been thinking. The whole trouble with Gloria is that she thinks of Robbie as a *person* and not as a *machine*. Naturally, she can't forget him. Now if we managed to convince her that Robbie was nothing more than a mess of steel and copper in the form of sheets and wires with electricity its juice of life, how long would her longings last? It's the psychological attack, if you see my point."

"How do you plan to do it?"

"Simple. Where do you suppose I went last night? I persuaded Robertson of U.S. Robots and Mechanical Men Corporation to arrange for a complete tour of his premises tomorrow. The three of us will go, and by the time we're through, Gloria will have it drilled into her that a robot is *not* alive."

Mrs. Weston's eyes widened gradually and something glinted in her eyes that was quite like sudden admiration, "Why, George, that's a *good* idea."

And George Weston's vest buttons strained. "Only kind I have," he said.

Mr. Struthers was a conscientious General Manager and naturally inclined to be a bit talkative. The combination, therefore, resulted in a tour that was fully explained, perhaps even overabundantly explained, at every step. However, Mrs. Weston was not bored. Indeed, she stopped him several times and begged him to repeat his statements in simpler language so that Gloria might understand. Under the influence of this appreciation of his narrative powers, Mr. Struthers expanded genially and became ever more communicative, if possible.

George Weston, himself, showed a gathering impatience.

"Pardon me, Struthers," he said, breaking into the middle of a lecture on the photo-electric cell, "haven't you a section of the factory where only robot labor is employed?"

"Eh? Oh, yes! Yes, indeed!" He smiled at Mrs. Weston. "A vicious circle in a way, robots creating more robots. Of course, we are not making a general practice out of it. For one thing, the unions would never let us. But we can turn out a very few robots using robot labor exclusively, merely as a sort of scientific experiment. You see," he tapped his pince-nez into one palm argumentatively, "what the labor unions don't realize—and I say this as a man who has always been very sympathetic with the labor movement in general—is that the advent of the robot, while involving some dislocation to begin with, will, inevitably—"

"Yes, Struthers," said Weston, "but about that section of the factory you speak of—may we see it? It would be very interesting, I'm sure."

"Yes! Yes, of course!" Mr. Struthers replaced his pince-nez in one convulsive movement and gave vent to a soft cough of discomfiture. "Follow me, please."

He was comparatively quiet while leading the three through a long corridor and down a flight of stairs. Then, when they had entered a large well-lit room that buzzed with metallic activity, the sluices opened and the flood of explanation poured forth again.

"There you are!" he said with pride in his voice. "Robots only! Five men act as overseers and they don't even stay in this room. In five years, that is, since we began this project, not a single accident has occurred. Of course, the robots here assembled are comparatively simple, but . . ."

The General Manager's voice had long died to a rather soothing murmur in Gloria's ears. The whole trip seemed rather dull and pointless to her, though there *were* many robots in sight. None were even remotely like Robbie, though, and she surveyed them with open contempt.

In this room, there weren't any people at all, she noticed. Then her eyes fell upon six or seven robots busily engaged at a round table halfway across the room. They widened in incredulous surprise. It was a big room. She couldn't see for sure, but one of the robots looked like—looked like—*it was!*

"*Robbie!*" Her shriek pierced the air, and one of the robots about the table faltered and dropped the tool he was holding. Gloria went almost mad with joy. Squeezing through the railing before either parent could stop her, she dropped lightly to the floor a few feet below, and ran toward her Robbie, arms waving and hair flying.

And the three horrified adults, as they stood frozen in their tracks, saw what the excited little girl did not see,—a huge, lumbering tractor bearing blindly down upon its appointed track.

It took split-seconds for Weston to come to his senses, and those split-seconds meant everything, for Gloria could not be overtaken. Although Weston vaulted the railing in a wild attempt, it was obviously hopeless. Mr. Struthers signalled wildly to the overseers to stop the tractor, but the overseers were only human and it took time to act.

It was only Robbie that acted immediately and with precision.

With metal legs eating up the space between himself and his little mistress he charged down from the opposite direction. Everything then happened at once. With one sweep of an arm, Robbie snatched up Gloria, slackening his speed not one iota, and, consequently, knocking every breath of air out of her. Weston, not quite comprehending all that was happening, felt, rather than saw, Robbie brush past him, and came to a sudden bewildered halt. The tractor intersected Gloria's path half a second after Robbie had, rolled on ten feet further and came to a grinding, long-drawn-out stop.

Gloria regained her breath, submitted to a series of passionate hugs on the part of both her parents and turned eagerly toward Robbie. As far as she was concerned, nothing had happened except that she had found her friend.

But Mrs. Weston's expression had changed from one of relief to one of dark suspicion. She turned to her husband, and, despite her disheveled and undignified appearance, managed to look quite formidable, "*You* engineered this, *didn't* you?"

George Weston swabbed at a hot forehead with his handkerchief. His hand was unsteady, and his lips could curve only into a tremulous and exceedingly weak smile.

Mrs. Weston pursued the thought, "Robbie wasn't designed for engineering or construction work. He couldn't be of any use to them. You had him placed there deliberately so that Gloria would find him. You know you did."

"Well, I did," said Weston. "But, Grace, how was I to know the reunion would be so violent? And Robbie has saved her life; you'll have to admit that. You *can't* send him away again."

Grace Weston considered. She turned toward Gloria and Robbie and watched them abstractedly for a moment. Gloria had a grip about the robot's neck that would have asphyxiated any creature but one of metal, and was prattling nonsense in half-hysterical frenzy. Robbie's chrome-steel arms (capable of bending a bar of steel two inches in diameter into a pretzel) wound about the little girl gently and lovingly, and his eyes glowed a deep, deep red.

"Well," said Mrs. Weston, at last, "I guess he can stay with us until he rusts."

NIGHTFALL

"If the stars should appear one night in a thousand years, how would men believe and adore, and preserve for many generations the remembrance of the city of God?"

EMERSON

Aton 77, director of Saro University, thrust out a belligerent lower lip and glared at the young newspaperman in a hot fury.

Theremon 762 took that fury in his stride. In his earlier days, when his now widely syndicated column was only a mad idea in a cub reporter's mind, he had specialized in "impossible" interviews. It had cost him bruises, black eyes, and broken bones; but it had given him an ample supply of coolness and self-confidence.

So he lowered the outthrust hand that had been so pointedly ignored and calmly waited for the aged director to get over the worst. Astronomers were queer ducks, anyway, and if Aton's actions of the last two months meant anything, this same Aton was the queer-duckiest of the lot.

Aton 77 found his voice, and though it trembled with restrained emotion, the careful, somewhat pedantic phraseology, for which the famous astronomer was noted, did not abandon him.

"Sir," he said, "you display an infernal gall in coming to me with that impudent proposition of yours."

The husky telephotographer of the Observatory, Beenay 25, thrust a tongue's tip across dry lips and interposed nervously, "Now, sir, after all—"

The director turned to him and lifted a white eyebrow. "Do not interfere, Beenay. I will credit you with good intentions in bringing this man here; but I will tolerate no insubordination now."

Theremon decided it was time to take a part. "Director Aton, if you'll let me finish what I started saying, I think—"

"I don't believe, young man," retorted Aton, "that anything you could say now would count for much as compared with your daily columns of these last two months. You have led a vast newspaper campaign against the efforts of myself and my colleagues to organize the world against the menace which it is now too late to avert. You have done your best with your highly personal attacks to make the staff of this Observatory objects of ridicule."

The director lifted a copy of the Saro City *Chronicle* from the table and shook it at Theremon furiously. "Even a person of your well-known impudence should have hesitated before coming to me with a request that he be allowed to cover today's events for his paper. Of all newsmen, you!"

Aton dashed the newspaper to the floor, strode to the window, and clasped his arms behind his back.

"You may leave," he snapped over his shoulder. He stared moodily out at the skyline where Gamma, the brightest of the planet's six suns, was setting. It had already faded and yellowed into the horizon mists, and Aton knew he would never see it again as a sane man.

He whirled. "No, wait, come here!" He gestured peremptorily. "I'll give you your story."

The newsman had made no motion to leave, and now he approached the old man slowly. Aton gestured outward. "Of the six suns, only Beta is left in the sky. Do you see it?"

The question was rather unnecessary. Beta was almost at zenith, its ruddy light flooding the landscape to an unusual orange as the brilliant rays of setting Gamma died. Beta was at aphelion. It was small; smaller than Theremon had ever seen it before, and for the moment it was undisputed ruler of Lagash's sky.

Lagash's own sun, Alpha, the one about which it revolved, was at the antipodes, as were the two distant companion pairs. The red dwarf Beta—Alpha's immediate companion—was alone, grimly alone.

Aton's upturned face flushed redly in the sunlight. "In just under four hours," he said, "civilization, as we know it, comes to an end. It will do so because, as you see, Beta is the only sun in the sky." He smiled grimly. "Print that! There'll be no one to read it."

"But if it turns out that four hours pass—and another four—and nothing happens?" asked Theremon softly.

"Don't let that worry you. Enough will happen."

"Granted! And, *still*—if nothing happens?"

For a second time, Beenay 25 spoke. "Sir, I think you ought to listen to him."

Theremon said, "Put it to a vote, Director Aton."

There was a stir among the remaining five members of the Observatory staff, who till now had maintained an attitude of wary neutrality.

"That," stated Aton flatly, "is not necessary." He drew out his pocket watch. "Since your good friend, Beenay, insists so urgently, I will give you five minutes. Talk away."

"Good! Now, just what difference would it make if you allowed me to take down an eyewitness account of what's to come? If your prediction comes true, my presence won't hurt; for in that case my column would never be written. On the other hand, if nothing comes of it, you will just have to expect ridicule or worse. It would be wise to leave that ridicule to friendly hands."

Aton snorted. "Do you mean yours when you speak of friendly hands?"

"Certainly!" Theremon sat down and crossed his legs. "My columns may have been a little rough, but I gave you people the benefit of the doubt every time. After all, this is not the century to preach 'The end of the world is at hand' to Lagash. You have to understand that people don't believe the *Book of Revelations* anymore, and it annoys them to have scientists turn about-face and tell us the Cultists are right after all—"

"No such thing, young man," interrupted Aton. "While a great deal of our data has been supplied us by the Cult, our results contain none of the Cult's mysticism. Facts are facts, and the Cult's so-called mythology *has* certain facts behind it. We've exposed them and ripped away their mystery. I assure you that the Cult hates us now worse than you do."

"I don't hate you. I'm just trying to tell you that the public is in an ugly humor. They're angry."

Aton twisted his mouth in derision. "Let them be angry."

"Yes, but what about tomorrow?"

"There'll be no tomorrow!"

"But if there is. Say that there is—just to see what happens. That anger might take shape into something serious. After all, you know, business has taken a nosedive these last two months. Investors don't really believe the world is coming to an end, but just the same they're being cagy with their money until it's all over. Johnny Public doesn't believe you, either, but the new spring furniture might just as well wait a few months—just to make sure.

"You see the point. Just as soon as this is all over, the business interests will be after your hide. They'll say that if crackpots—begging your pardon—can upset the country's prosperity any time they want, simply by making some cockeyed prediction—it's up to the planet to prevent them. The sparks will fly, sir."

The director regarded the columnist sternly. "And just what were you proposing to do to help the situation?"

"Well"—Theremon grinned—"I was proposing to take charge of the publicity. I can handle things so that only the ridiculous side will show. It would be hard to stand, I admit, because I'd have to make you all out to be a bunch of gibbering idiots, but if I can get people laughing at you, they might forget to be angry. In return for that, all my publisher asks is an exclusive story."

Beenay nodded and burst out, "Sir, the rest of us think he's right. These last two months we've considered everything but the million-to-one chance that there is an error somewhere in our theory or in our calculations. We ought to take care of that, too."

There was a murmur of agreement from the men grouped about the table, and Aton's expression became that of one who found his mouth full of something bitter and couldn't get rid of it.

"You may stay if you wish, then. You will kindly refrain, however, from hampering us in our duties in any way. You will also remember that I am in charge of all activities here, and in spite of your opinions as expressed in your columns, I will expect full cooperation and full respect—"

His hands were behind his back, and his wrinkled face thrust forward determinedly as he spoke. He might have continued indefinitely but for the intrusion of a new voice.

"Hello, hello, hello!" It came in a high tenor, and the plump cheeks of the newcomer expanded in a pleased smile. "What's this morgue-like atmosphere about here? No one's losing his nerve, I hope."

Aton started in consternation and said peevishly, "Now what the devil are you doing here, Sheerin? I thought you were going to stay behind in the Hideout."

Sheerin laughed and dropped his tubby figure into a chair. "Hideout be blowed! The place bored me. I wanted to be here, where things are getting hot. Don't you suppose I have my share of curiosity? I want to see these Stars the Cultists are forever speaking about." He rubbed his hands and added in a soberer tone, "It's freezing outside. The wind's enough to hang icicles on your nose. Beta doesn't seem to give any heat at all, at the distance it is."

The white-haired director ground his teeth in sudden exasperation. "Why do you go out of your way to do crazy things, Sheerin? What kind of good are you around here?"

"What kind of good am I around there?" Sheerin spread his palms in comical resignation. "A psychologist isn't worth his salt in the Hideout. They need men of action and strong, healthy women that can breed children. Me? I'm a hundred pounds too heavy for a man of action, and I wouldn't be a success at breeding children. So why bother them with an extra mouth to feed? I feel better over here."

Theremon spoke briskly. "Just what is the Hideout, sir?"

Sheerin seemed to see the columnist for the first time. He frowned and blew his ample cheeks out. "And just who in Lagash are you, redhead?"

Aton compressed his lips and then muttered sullenly, "That's Theremon 762, the newspaper fellow. I suppose you've heard of him."

The columnist offered his hand. "And, of course, you're Sheerin 501 of Saro University. I've heard of you." Then he repeated, "What is this Hideout, sir?"

"Well," said Sheerin, "we have managed to convince a few people of the validity of our prophecy of—er—doom, to be spectacular about it, and those few have taken proper measures. They consist mainly of the immediate members of the families of the Observatory staff, certain of the faculty of Saro University, and a few outsiders. Altogether, they number about three hundred, but three quarters are women and children."

"I see! They're supposed to hide where the Darkness and the—er—Stars can't get at them, and then hold out when the rest of the world goes poof."

"If they can. It won't be easy. With all of mankind insane, with the great cities going up in flames— environment will not be conducive to survival. But they have food, water, shelter, and weapons—"

"They've got more," said Aton. "They've got all our records, except for what we will collect today. Those records will mean everything to the next cycle, and *that's* what must survive. The rest can go hang."

Theremon uttered a long, low whistle and sat brooding for several minutes. The men about the table had brought out a multi-chess board and started a six-member game.

Moves were made rapidly and in silence. All eyes bent in furious concentration on the board. Theremon watched them intently and then rose and approached Aton, who sat apart in whispered conversation with Sheerin.

"Listen," he said, "let's go somewhere where we won't bother the rest of the fellows. I want to ask some questions."

The aged astronomer frowned sourly at him, but Sheerin chirped up, "Certainly. It will do me good to talk. It always does. Aton was telling me about your ideas concerning world reaction to a failure of the prediction—and I agree with you. I read your column pretty regularly, by the way, and as a general thing I like your views."

"Please, Sheerin," growled Aton.

"Eh? Oh, all right. We'll go into the next room. It has softer chairs, anyway."

There were softer chairs in the next room. There were also thick red curtains on the windows and a maroon carpet on the floor. With the bricky light of Beta pouring in, the general effect was one of dried blood.

Theremon shuddered. "Say, I'd give ten credits for a decent dose of white light for just a second. I wish Gamma or Delta were in the sky."

"What are your questions?" asked Aton. "Please remember that our time is limited. In a little over an hour and a quarter we're going upstairs, and after that there will be no time for talk."

"Well, here it is." Theremon leaned back and folded his hands on his chest. "You people seem so all-fired serious about this that I'm beginning to believe you. Would you mind explaining what it's all about?"

Aton exploded, "Do you mean to sit there and tell me that you've been bombarding us with ridicule without even finding out what we've been trying to say?"

The columnist grinned sheepishly. "It's not that bad, sir. I've got the general idea. You say there is going to be a world-wide Darkness in a few hours and that all mankind will go violently insane. What I want now is the science behind it."

"No, you don't. No, you don't," broke in Sheerin. "If you ask Aton for that—supposing him to be in the mood to answer at all—he'll trot out pages of figures and volumes of graphs. You won't make head or tail of it. Now if you were to ask me, I could give you the layman's standpoint."

"All right; I ask you."

"Then first I'd like a drink." He rubbed his hands and looked at Aton.

"Water?" grunted Aton.

"Don't be silly!"

"Don't you be silly. No alcohol today. It would be too easy to get my men drunk. I can't afford to tempt them."

The psychologist grumbled wordlessly. He turned to Theremon, impaled him with his sharp eyes, and began.

"You realize, of course, that the history of civilization on Lagash displays a cyclic character—but I mean, *cyclic!*"

"I know," replied Theremon cautiously, "that that is the current archaeological theory. Has it been accepted as a fact?"

"Just about. In this last century it's been generally agreed upon. This cyclic character is—or rather, was—one of the great mysteries. We've located series of civilizations, nine of them definitely, and indications of others as well, all of which have reached heights comparable to our own, and all of which, without exception, were destroyed by fire at the very height of their culture.

"And no one could tell why. All centers of culture were thoroughly gutted by fire, with nothing left behind to give a hint as to the cause."

Theremon was following closely. "Wasn't there a Stone Age, too?"

"Probably, but as yet practically nothing is known of it, except that men of that age were little more than rather intelligent apes. We can forget about that."

"I see. Go on!"

"There have been explanations of these recurrent catastrophes, all of a more or less fantastic nature. Some say that there are periodic rains of fire; some that Lagash passes through a sun every so often; some even wilder things. But there is one theory, quite different from all of these, that has been handed down over a period of centuries."

"I know. You mean this myth of the 'Stars' that the Cultists have in their *Book of Revelations*."

"Exactly," rejoined Sheerin with satisfaction. "The Cultists said that every two thousand and fifty years Lagash entered a huge cave, so that all the suns disappeared, and there came *total darkness all over the world!* And then, they say, things called Stars appeared, which robbed men of their souls and left them unreasoning brutes, so that they destroyed the civilization they themselves had built up. Of course they mix all this up with a lot of religio-mystic notions, but that's the central idea."

There was a short pause in which Sheerin drew a long breath. "And now we come to the Theory of Universal Gravitation." He pronounced the phrase so that the capital letters sounded—and at that point Aton turned from the window, snorted loudly, and stalked out of the room.

The two stared after him, and Theremon said, "What's wrong?"

"Nothing in particular," replied Sheerin. "Two of the men were due several hours ago and haven't shown up yet. He's terrifically short-handed, of course, because all but the really essential men have gone to the Hideout."

"You don't think the two deserted, do you?"

"Who? Faro and Yimot? Of course not. Still, if they're not back within the hour, things would be a little sticky." He got to his feet suddenly, and his eyes twinkled. "Anyway, as long as Aton is gone—"

Tiptoeing to the nearest window, he squatted, and from the low window box beneath withdrew a bottle of red liquid that gurgled suggestively when he shook it.

"I *thought* Aton didn't know about this," he remarked as

he trotted back to the table. "Here! We've only got one glass so, as the guest, you can have it. I'll keep the bottle." And he filled the tiny cup with judicious care.

Theremon rose to protest, but Sheerin eyed him sternly. "Respect your elders, young man."

The newsman seated himself with a look of anguish on his face. "Go ahead, then, you old villain."

The psychologist's Adam's apple wobbled as the bottle upended, and then, with a satisfied grunt and a smack of the lips, he began again. "But what do you know about gravitation?"

"Nothing, except that it is a very recent development, not too well established, and that the math is so hard that only twelve men in Lagash are supposed to understand it."

"*Tcha!* Nonsense! Baloney! I can give you all the essential math in a sentence. The Law of Universal Gravitation states that there exists a cohesive force among all bodies of the universe, such that the amount of this force between any two given bodies is proportional to the product of their masses divided by the square of the distance between them."

"Is that all?"

"That's enough! It took four hundred years to develop it."

"Why that long? It sounded simple enough, the way you said it."

"Because great laws are not divined by flashes of inspiration, whatever you may think. It usually takes the combined work of a world full of scientists over a period of centuries. After Genovi 41 discovered that Lagash rotated about the sun Alpha rather than vice versa—and that was four hundred years ago—astronomers have been working. The complex motions of the six suns were recorded and analyzed and unwoven. Theory after theory was advanced and checked and counterchecked and modified and abandoned and revived and converted to something else. It was a devil of a job."

Theremon nodded thoughtfully and held out his glass for more liquor. Sheerin grudgingly allowed a few ruby drops to leave the bottle.

"It was twenty years ago," he continued after remoistening his own throat, "that it was finally demonstrated that the Law of Universal Gravitation accounted exactly for the orbital motions of the six suns. It was a great triumph."

Sheerin stood up and walked to the window, still clutching his bottle. "And now we're getting to the point. In the last decade, the motions of Lagash about Alpha were computed according to gravity, and *it did not account for the orbit observed;* not even when all perturbations due to the other suns were included. Either the law was invalid, or there was another, as yet unknown, factor involved."

Theremon joined Sheerin at the window and gazed out past the wooded slopes to where the spires of Saro City gleamed bloodily on the horizon. The newsman felt the tension of uncertainty grow within him as he cast a short glance at Beta. It glowered redly at zenith, dwarfed and evil.

"Go ahead, sir," he said softly.

Sheerin replied, "Astronomers stumbled about for years, each proposed theory more untenable than the one before— until Aton had the inspiration of calling in the Cult. The head of the Cult, Sor 5, had access to certain data that simplified the problem considerably. Aton set to work on a new track.

"What if there were another nonluminous planetary body such as Lagash? If there were, you know, it would shine only by reflected light, and if it were composed of bluish rock, as Lagash itself largely is, then, in the redness of the sky, the eternal blaze of the suns would make it invisible— drown it out completely."

Theremon whistled. "What a screwy idea!"

"You think *that's* screwy? Listen to this: Suppose this body rotated about Lagash at such a distance and in such an orbit and had such a mass that its attraction would exactly

account for the deviations of Lagash's orbit from theory—
do you know what would happen?"

The columnist shook his head.

"Well, sometimes this body would get in the way of a
sun." And Sheerin emptied what remained in the bottle at a
draft.

"And it does, I suppose," said Theremon flatly.

"Yes! But only one sun lies in its plane of revolution."
He jerked a thumb at the shrunken sun above. "Beta! And
it had been shown that the eclipse will occur only when the
arrangement of the suns is such that Beta is alone in its
hemisphere and at maximum distance, at which time the
moon is invariably at minimum distance. The eclipse that
results, with the moon seven times the apparent diameter of
Beta, covers all of Lagash and lasts well over a half a day,
so that no spot on the planet escapes the effects. *That eclipse
comes once every two thousand and forty-nine years.*"

Theremon's face was drawn into an expressionless mask.
"And that's my story?"

The psychologist nodded. "That's all of it. First the
eclipse—which will start in three quarters of an hour—then
universal Darkness and, maybe, these mysterious Stars—
then madness, and end of the cycle."

He brooded. "We had two months' leeway—we at the
Observatory—and that wasn't enough time to persuade
Lagash of the danger. Two centuries might not have been
enough. But our records are at the Hideout, and today we
photograph the eclipse. The next cycle will *start off* with the
truth, and when the *next* eclipse comes, mankind will at last
be ready for it. Come to think of it, that's part of your story
too."

A thin wind ruffled the curtains at the window as
Theremon opened it and leaned out. It played coldly with
his hair as he stared at the crimson sunlight on his hand.
Then he turned in sudden rebellion.

"What is there in Darkness to drive *me* mad?"

Sheerin smiled to himself as he spun the empty liquor

bottle with abstracted motions of his hand. "Have you ever experienced Darkness, young man?"

The newsman leaned against the wall and considered. "No. Can't say I have. But I know what it is. Just—uh—" He made vague motions with his fingers and then brightened. "Just no light. Like in caves."

"Have you ever been in a cave?"

"In a *cave!* Of course not!"

"I thought not. *I* tried last week—just to see—but I got out in a hurry. I went in until the mouth of the cave was just visible as a blur of light, with black everywhere else. I never thought a person my weight could run that fast."

Theremon's lip curled. "Well, if it comes to that, I guess I wouldn't have run if I had been there."

The psychologist studied the young man with an annoyed frown.

"My, don't you talk big! I dare you to draw the curtain."

Theremon looked his surprise and said, "What for? If we had four or five suns out there, we might want to cut the light down a bit for comfort, but now we haven't enough light as it is."

"That's the point. Just draw the curtain; then come here and sit down."

"All right." Theremon reached for the tasseled string and jerked. The red curtain slid across the wide window, the brass rings hissing their way along the crossbar, and a dusk-red shadow clamped down on the room.

Theremon's footsteps sounded hollowly in the silence as he made his way to the table, and then they stopped halfway. "I can't see you, sir," he whispered.

"Feel your way," ordered Sheerin in a strained voice.

"But I can't see you, sir." The newsman was breathing harshly. "I can't see anything."

"What did you expect?" came the grim reply. "Come here and sit down!"

The footsteps sounded again, waveringly, approaching slowly. There was the sound of someone fumbling with a chair. Theremon's voice came thinly, "Here I am. I feel . . . *ulp* . . . all right."

"You like it, do you?"

"N—no. It's pretty awful. The walls seem to be—" He paused. "They seem to be closing in on me. I keep wanting to push them away. But I'm not going *mad!* In fact, the feeling isn't as bad as it was."

"All right. Draw the curtain back again."

There were cautious footsteps through the dark, the rustle of Theremon's body against the curtain as he felt for the tassel, and then the triumphant *ro-o-osh* of the curtain slithering back. Red light flooded the room, and with a cry of joy Theremon looked up at the sun.

Sheerin wiped the moistness off his forehead with the back of a hand and said shakily, "And that was just a dark room."

"It can be stood," said Theremon lightly.

"Yes, a dark room can. But were you at the Jonglor Centennial Exposition two years ago?"

"No, it so happens I never got around to it. Six thousand miles was just a bit too much to travel, even for the exposition."

"Well, I was there. You remember hearing about the 'Tunnel of Mystery' that broke all records in the amusement area—for the first month or so, anyway?"

"Yes. Wasn't there some fuss about it?"

"Very little. It was hushed up. You see, that Tunnel of Mystery was just a mile-long tunnel—with no lights. You got into a little open car and jolted along through Darkness for fifteen minutes. It was very popular—while it lasted."

"Popular?"

"Certainly. There's a fascination in being frightened *when it's part of a game*. A baby is born with three instinctive fears: of loud noises, of falling, and of the absence of light. That's why it's considered so funny to jump at someone and shout 'Boo!' That's why it's such fun to ride a roller coaster. And that's why that Tunnel of

Mystery started cleaning up. People came out of that Darkness shaking, breathless, half dead with fear, but they kept on paying to get in."

"Wait a while, I remember now. Some people came out dead, didn't they? There were rumors of that after it shut down."

The psychologist snorted. "Bah! Two or three died. That was nothing! They paid off the families of the dead ones and argued the Jonglor City Council into forgetting it. After all, they said, if people with weak hearts want to go through the tunnel, it was at their own risk—and besides, it wouldn't happen again. So they put a doctor in the front office and had every customer go through a physical examination before getting into the car. That actually *boosted* ticket sales."

"Well, then?"

"But you see, there was something else. People sometimes came out in perfect order, except that they refused to go into buildings—any buildings; including palaces, mansions, apartment houses, tenements, cottages, huts, shacks, lean-tos, and tents."

Theremon looked shocked. "You mean they refused to come in out of the open? Where'd they sleep?"

"In the open."

"They should have *forced* them inside."

"Oh, they did, they did. Whereupon these people went into violent hysterics and did their best to bat their brains out against the nearest wall. Once you got them inside, you couldn't keep them there without a strait jacket or a heavy dose of tranquilizer."

"They must have been crazy."

"Which is exactly what they were. One person out of every ten who went into that tunnel came out that way. They called in the psychologists, and we did the only thing possible. We closed down the exhibit." He spread his hands.

"What was the matter with these people?" asked Theremon finally.

"Essentially the same thing that was the matter with you when you thought the walls of the room were crushing in on you in the dark. There is a psychological term for mankind's instinctive fear of the absence of light. We call it 'claustrophobia,' because the lack of light is always tied up with enclosed places, so that fear of one is fear of the other. You see?"

"And those people of the tunnel?"

"Those people of the tunnel consisted of those unfortunates whose mentality did not quite possess the resiliency to overcome the claustrophobia that overtook them in the Darkness. Fifteen minutes without light is a long time; you only had two or three minutes, and I believe you were fairly upset.

"The people of the tunnel had what is called a 'claustrophobic fixation.' Their latent fear of Darkness and enclosed places had crystallized and become active, and, as far as we can tell, permanent. That's what fifteen minutes in the dark will do."

There was a long silence, and Theremon's forehead wrinkled slowly into a frown. "I don't believe it's that bad."

"You mean you don't want to believe," snapped Sheerin. "You're afraid to believe. Look out the window!"

Theremon did so, and the psychologist continued without pausing. "Imagine Darkness—everywhere. No light, as far as you can see. The houses, the trees, the fields, the earth, the sky—black! And Stars thrown in, for all I know—whatever *they* are. Can you conceive it?"

"Yes, I can," declared Theremon truculently.

And Sheerin slammed his fist down upon the table in sudden passion. "You lie! You can't conceive that. Your brain wasn't built for the conception any more than it was built for the conception of infinity or of eternity. You can only talk about it. A fraction of the reality upsets you, and when the real thing comes, your brain is going to be presented with the phenomenon outside its limits of comprehension. You will go mad, completely and permanently! There is no question of it!"

He added sadly, "And another couple of millennia of painful struggle comes to nothing. Tomorrow there won't be a city standing unharmed in all Lagash."

Theremon recovered part of his mental equilibrium. "That doesn't follow. I still don't see that I can go loony just because there isn't a sun in the sky—but even if I did, and everyone else did, how does that harm the cities? Are we going to blow them down?"

But Sheerin was angry, too. "If you were in Darkness, what would you want more than anything else; what would it be that every instinct would call for? Light, damn you, *light!*"

"Well?"

"And how would you get light?"

"I don't know," said Theremon flatly.

"What's the *only* way to get light, short of a sun?"

"How should I know?"

They were standing face to face and nose to nose.

Sheerin said, "You burn something, mister. Ever see a forest fire? Ever go camping and cook a stew over a wood fire? Heat isn't the only thing burning wood gives off, you know. It gives off light, and people know that. And when it's dark they want light, and they're going to *get* it."

"So they burn wood?"

"So they burn whatever they can get. They've got to have light. They've got to burn something, and wood isn't handy—so they'll burn whatever is nearest. They'll have their light—and every center of habitation goes up in flames!"

Eyes held each other as though the whole matter were a personal affair of respective will powers, and then Theremon broke away wordlessly. His breathing was harsh and ragged, and he scarcely noted the sudden hubbub that came from the adjoining room behind the closed door.

Sheerin spoke, and it was with an effort that he made it sound matter-of-fact. "I think I heard Yimot's voice. He and Faro are probably back. Let's go in and see what kept them."

"Might as well!" muttered Theremon. He drew a long breath and seemed to shake himself. The tension was broken.

The room was in an uproar, with members of the staff clustering about two young men who were removing outer garments even as they parried the miscellany of questions being thrown at them.

Aton bustled through the crowd and faced the newcomers angrily. "Do you realize that it's less than half an hour before deadline? Where have you two been?"

Faro 24 seated himself and rubbed his hands. His cheeks were red with the outdoor chill. "Yimot and I have just finished carrying through a little crazy experiment of our own. We've been trying to see if we couldn't construct an arrangement by which we could simulate the appearance of Darkness and Stars so as to get an advance notion as to how it looked."

There was a confused murmur from the listeners, and a sudden look of interest entered Aton's eyes. "There wasn't anything said of this before. How did you go about it?"

"Well," said Faro, "the idea came to Yimot and myself long ago, and we've been working it out in our spare time. Yimot knew of a low one-story house down in the city with a domed roof—it had once been used as a museum, I think. Anyway, we bought it—"

"Where did you get the money?" interrupted Aton peremptorily.

"Our bank accounts," grunted Yimot 70. "It cost two thousand credits." Then, defensively, "Well, what of it? Tomorrow, two thousand credits will be two thousand pieces of paper. That's all."

"Sure," agreed Faro. "We bought the place and rigged it

up with black velvet from top to bottom so as to get as perfect a Darkness as possible. Then we punched tiny holes in the ceiling and through the roof and covered them with little metal caps, all of which could be shoved aside simultaneously at the close of a switch. At least we didn't do that part ourselves; we got a carpenter and an electrician and some others—money didn't count. The point was that we could get the light to shine through those holes in the roof, so that we could get a starlike effect."

Not a breath was drawn during the pause that followed. Aton said stiffly, "You had no right to make a private—"

Faro seemed abashed. "I know, sir—but frankly, Yimot and I thought the experiment was a little dangerous. If the effect really worked, we half expected to go mad—from what Sheerin says about all this, we thought that would be rather likely. We wanted to take the risk ourselves. Of course if we found we could retain sanity, it occurred to us that we might develop immunity to the real thing, and then expose the rest of you the same way. But things didn't work out at all—"

"Why, what happened?"

It was Yimot who answered. "We shut ourselves in and allowed our eyes to get accustomed to the dark. It's an extremely creepy feeling because the total Darkness makes you feel as if the walls and ceiling are crushing in on you. But we got over that and pulled the switch. The caps fell away and the roof glittered all over with little dots of light—"

"Well?"

"Well—nothing. That was the whacky part of it. Nothing happened. It was just a roof with holes in it, and that's just what it looked like. We tried it over and over again—that's what kept us so late—but there just isn't any effect at all."

There followed a shocked silence, and all eyes turned to Sheerin, who sat motionless, mouth open.

Theremon was the first to speak. "You know what this

does to this whole theory you've built up, Sheerin, don't you?" He was grinning with relief.

But Sheerin raised his hand. "Now wait a while. Just let me think this through." And then he snapped his fingers, and when he lifted his head there was neither surprise nor uncertainty in his eyes. "Of course—"

He never finished. From somewhere up above there sounded a sharp clang, and Beenay, starting to his feet, dashed up the stairs with a "What the devil!"

The rest followed after.

Things happened quickly. Once up in the dome, Beenay cast one horrified glance at the shattered photographic plates and at the man bending over them; and then hurled himself fiercely at the intruder, getting a death grip on his throat. There was a wild threshing, and as others of the staff joined in, the stranger was swallowed up and smothered under the weight of half a dozen angry men.

Aton came up last, breathing heavily. "Let him up!"

There was a reluctant unscrambling and the stranger, panting harshly, with his clothes torn and his forehead bruised, was hauled to his feet. He had a short yellow beard curled elaborately in the style affected by the Cultists.

Beenay shifted his hold to a collar grip and shook the man savagely. "All right, rat, what's the idea? These plates—"

"I wasn't after *them*," retorted the Cultist coldly. "That was an accident."

Beenay followed his glowering stare and snarled, "I see. You were after the cameras themselves. The accident with the plates was a stroke of luck for you, then. If you had touched Snapping Bertha or any of the others, you would have died by slow torture. As it is—" He drew his fist back.

Aton grabbed his sleeve. "Stop that! Let him go!"

The young technician wavered, and his arm dropped reluctantly. Aton pushed him aside and confronted the Cultist. "You're Latimer, aren't you?"

The Cultist bowed stiffly and indicated the symbol upon

his hip. "I am Latimer 25, adjutant of the third class to his serenity, Sor 5."

"And"—Aton's white eyebrows lifted—"you were with his serenity when he visited me last week, weren't you?"

Latimer bowed a second time.

"Now, then, what do you want?"

"Nothing that you would give me of your own free will."

"Sor 5 sent you, I suppose—or is this your own idea?"

"I won't answer that question."

"Will there be any further visitors?"

"I won't answer that, either."

Aton glanced at his timepiece and scowled. "Now, man, what is it your master wants of me? I have fulfilled my end of the bargain."

Latimer smiled faintly, but said nothing.

"I asked him," continued Aton angrily, "for data only the Cult could supply, and it was given to me. For that, thank you. In return I promised to prove the essential truth of the creed of the Cult."

"There was no need to prove that," came the proud retort. "It stands proven by the *Book of Revelations*."

"For the handful that constitute the Cult, yes. Don't pretend to mistake my meaning. I offered to present scientific backing for your beliefs. And I did!"

The Cultist's eyes narrowed bitterly. "Yes, you did— with a fox's subtlety, for your pretended explanation backed our beliefs, and at the same time removed all necessity for them. You made of the Darkness and of the Stars a natural phenomenon and removed all its real significance. That was blasphemy."

"If so, the fault isn't mine. The facts exist. What can I do but state them?"

"Your 'facts' are a fraud and a delusion."

Aton stamped angrily. "How do you know?"

And the answer came with the certainty of absolute faith. "I know!"

The director purpled and Beenay whispered urgently.

Aton waved him silent. "And what does Sor 5 want us to do? He still thinks, I suppose, that in trying to warn the world to take measures against the menace of madness, we are placing innumerable souls in jeopardy. We aren't succeeding, if that means anything to him."

"The attempt itself has done harm enough, and your vicious effort to gain information by means of your devilish instruments must be stopped. We obey the will of the Stars, and I only regret that my clumsiness prevented me from wrecking your infernal devices."

"It wouldn't have done you too much good," returned Aton. "All our data, except for the direct evidence we intend collecting right now, is already safely cached and well beyond possibility of harm." He smiled grimly. "But that does not affect your present status as an attempted burglar and criminal."

He turned to the men behind him. "Someone call the police at Saro City."

There was a cry of distaste from Sheerin. "Damn it, Aton, what's wrong with you? There's no time for that. Here"—he bustled his way forward—"let me handle this."

Aton stared down his nose at the psychologist. "This is not the time for your monkeyshines, Sheerin. Will you please let me handle this my own way? Right now you are a complete outsider here, and don't forget it."

Sheerin's mouth twisted eloquently. "Now why should we go to the impossible trouble of calling the police—with Beta's eclipse a matter of minutes from now—when this young man here is perfectly willing to pledge his word of honor to remain and cause no trouble whatsoever?"

The Cultist answered promptly, "I will do no such thing. You're free to do what you want, but it's only fair to warn you that just as soon as I get my chance I'm going to finish what I came out here to do. If it's my word of honor you're relying on, you'd better call the police."

Sheerin smiled in a friendly fashion. "You're a determined cuss, aren't you? Well, I'll explain something. Do you see that young man at the window? He's a strong, husky fellow, quite handy with his fists, and he's an outsider besides. Once the eclipse starts there will be nothing for him to do except keep an eye on you. Besides him, there will be myself—a little too stout for active fisticuffs, but still able to help."

"Well, what of it?" demanded Latimer frozenly.

"Listen and I'll tell you," was the reply. "Just as soon as the eclipse starts, we're going to take you, Theremon and I, and deposit you in a little closet with one door, to which is attached one giant lock and no windows. You will remain there for the duration."

"And afterward," breathed Latimer fiercely, "there'll be no one to let me out. I know as well as you do what the coming of the Stars means—I know it far better than you. With all your minds gone, you are not likely to free me. Suffocation or slow starvation, is it? About what I might have expected from a group of scientists. But I don't give my word. It's a matter of principle, and I won't discuss it further."

Aton seemed perturbed. His faded eyes were troubled. "Really, Sheerin, locking him—"

"Please!" Sheerin motioned him impatiently to silence. "I don't think for a moment things will go that far. Latimer has just tried a clever little bluff, but I'm not a psychologist just because I like the sound of the word." He grinned at the Cultist. "Come now, you don't really think I'm trying anything as crude as slow starvation. My dear Latimer, if I lock you in the closet, you are not going to see the Darkness, and you are not going to see the Stars. It does not take much knowledge of the fundamental creed of the Cult to realize that for you to be hidden from the Stars when they appear means the loss of your immortal soul. Now, I believe you to be an honorable man. I'll accept your word of honor to make no further effort to disrupt proceedings, if you'll offer it."

A vein throbbed in Latimer's temple, and he seemed to

shrink within himself as he said thickly, "You have it!" And then he added with swift fury, "But it is my consolation that you will all be damned for your deeds of today." He turned on his heel and stalked to the high three-legged stool by the door.

Sheerin nodded to the columnist. "Take a seat next to him, Theremon—just as a formality. Hey, Theremon!"

But the newspaperman didn't move. He had gone pale to the lips. "Look at that!" The finger he pointed toward the sky shook, and his voice was dry and cracked.

There was one simultaneous gasp as every eye followed the pointing finger and, for one breathless moment, stared frozenly.

Beta was chipped on one side!

The tiny bit of encroaching blackness was perhaps the width of a fingernail, but to the staring watchers it magnified itself into the crack of doom.

Only for a moment they watched, and after that there was a shrieking confusion that was even shorter of duration and which gave way to an orderly scurry of activity—each man at his prescribed job. At the crucial moment there was no time for emotion. The men were merely scientists with work to do. Even Aton had melted away.

Sheerin said prosaically, "First contact must have been made fifteen minutes ago. A little early, but pretty good considering the uncertainties involved in the calculation." He looked about him and then tiptoed to Theremon, who still remained staring out the window, and dragged him away gently.

"Aton is furious," he whispered, "so stay away. He missed first contact on account of this fuss with Latimer, and if you get in his way he'll have you thrown out the window."

Theremon nodded shortly and sat down. Sheerin stared in surprise at him.

"The devil, man," he exclaimed, "you're shaking."

"Eh?" Theremon licked dry lips and then tried to smile. "I don't feel very well, and that's a fact."

The psychologist's eyes hardened. "You're not losing your nerve?"

"No!" cried Theremon in a flash of indignation. "Give me a chance, will you? I haven't really believed this rigmarole—not way down beneath, anyway—till just this minute. Give me a chance to get used to the idea. You've been preparing yourself for two months or more."

"You're right, at that," replied Sheerin thoughtfully. "Listen! Have you got a family—parents, wife, children?"

Theremon shook his head. "You mean the Hideout, I suppose. No, you don't have to worry about that. I have a sister, but she's two thousand miles away. I don't even know her exact address."

"Well, then, what about yourself? You've got time to get there, and they're one short anyway, since I left. After all, you're not needed here, and you'd make a darned fine addition—"

Theremon looked at the other wearily. "You think I'm scared stiff, don't you? Well, get this, mister, I'm a newspaperman and I've been assigned to cover a story. I intend covering it."

There was a faint smile on the psychologist's face. "I see. Professional honor, is that it?"

"You might call it that. But, man, I'd give my right arm for another bottle of that sockeroo juice even half the size of the one you hogged. If ever a fellow needed a drink, I do."

He broke off. Sheerin was nudging him violently. "Do you hear that? Listen!"

Theremon followed the motion of the other's chin and stared at the Cultist, who, oblivious to all about him, faced the window, a look of wild elation on his face, droning to himself the while in singsong fashion.

"What's he saying?" whispered the columnist.

"He's quoting *Book of Revelations*, fifth chapter," replied Sheerin. Then, urgently, "Keep quiet and listen, I tell you."

The Cultist's voice had risen in a sudden increase of fervor: " 'And it came to pass that in those days the Sun, Beta, held lone vigil in the sky for ever longer periods as the revolutions passed; until such time as for full half a revolution, it alone, shrunken and cold, shone down upon Lagash.

" 'And men did assemble in the public squares and in the highways, there to debate and to marvel at the sight, for a strange depression had seized them. Their minds were troubled and their speech confused, for the souls of men awaited the coming of the Stars.

" 'And in the city of Trigon, at high noon, Vendret 2 came forth and said unto the men of Trigon, "Lo, ye sinners! Though ye scorn the ways of righteousness, yet will the time of reckoning come. Even now the Cave approaches to swallow Lagash; yea, and all it contains."

" 'And even as he spoke the lip of the Cave of Darkness passed the edge of Beta so that to all Lagash it was hidden from sight. Loud were the cries of men as it vanished, and great the fear of soul that fell upon them.

" 'It came to pass that the Darkness of the Cave fell upon Lagash, and there was no light on all the surface of Lagash. Men were even as blinded, nor could one man see his neighbor, though he felt his breath upon his face.

" 'And in this blackness there appeared the Stars, in countless numbers, and to the strains of music of such beauty that the very leaves of the trees cried out in wonder.

" 'And in that moment the souls of men departed from them, and their abandoned bodies became even as beasts; yea, even as brutes of the wild; so that through the blackened streets of the cities of Lagash they prowled with wild cries.

" 'From the Stars there then reached down the Heavenly Flame, and where it touched, the cities of Lagash flamed to utter destruction, so that of man and of the works of man nought remained.

" 'Even then—' "

There was a subtle change in Latimer's tone. His eyes had not shifted, but somehow he had become aware of the absorbed attention of the other two. Easily, without pausing for breath, the timbre of his voice shifted and the syllables became more liquid.

Theremon, caught by surprise, stared. The words seemed on the border of familiarity. There was an elusive shift in the accent, a tiny change in the vowel stress; nothing more—yet Latimer had become thoroughly unintelligible.

Sheerin smiled slyly. "He shifted to some old-cycle tongue, probably their traditional second cycle. That was the language in which the *Book of Revelations* was originally written, you know."

"It doesn't matter; I've heard enough." Theremon shoved his chair back and brushed his hair back with hands that no longer shook. "I feel much better now."

"You do?" Sheerin seemed mildly surprised.

"I'll say I do. I had a bad case of jitters just a while back. Listening to you and your gravitation and seeing that eclipse start almost finished me. But this"—he jerked a contemptuous thumb at the yellow-bearded Cultist—"*this* is the sort of thing my nurse used to tell me. I've been laughing at that sort of thing all my life. I'm not going to let it scare me *now*."

He drew a deep breath and said with a hectic gaiety, "But if I expect to keep on the good side of myself, I'm going to turn my chair away from the window."

Sheerin said, "Yes, but you'd better talk lower. Aton just lifted his head out of that box he's got it stuck into and gave you a look that should have killed you."

Theremon made a mouth. "I forgot about the old fellow." With elaborate care he turned the chair from the window, cast one distasteful look over his shoulder, and said, "It has occurred to me that there must be considerable immunity against this Star madness."

The psychologist did not answer immediately. Beta was past its zenith now, and the square of bloody sunlight that outlined the window upon the floor had lifted into Sheerin's lap. He stared at its dusky color thoughtfully and then bent and squinted into the sun itself.

The chip in its side had grown to a black encroachment that covered a third of Beta. He shuddered, and when he straightened once more his florid cheeks did not contain quite as much color as they had had previously.

With a smile that was almost apologetic, he reversed his chair also. "There are probably two million people in Saro City that are all trying to join the Cult at once in one gigantic revival." Then, ironically, "The Cult is in for an hour of unexampled prosperity. I trust they'll make the most of it. Now, what was it you said?"

"Just this. How did the Cultists manage to keep the *Book of Revelations* going from cycle to cycle, and how on Lagash did it get written in the first place? There must have been some sort of immunity, for if everyone had gone mad, who would be left to write the book?"

Sheerin stared at his questioner ruefully. "Well, now, young man, there isn't any eyewitness answer to that, but we've got a few damned good notions as to what happened. You see, there are three kinds of people who might remain relatively unaffected. First, the very few who don't see the Stars at all: the seriously retarded or those who drink themselves into a stupor at the beginning of the eclipse and remain so to the end. We leave them out—because they aren't really witnesses.

"Then there are children below six, to whom the world as a whole is too new and strange for them to be frightened at Stars and Darkness. They would be just another item in an already surprising world. You see that, don't you?"

The other nodded doubtfully. "I suppose so."

"Lastly, there are those whose minds are too coarsely

grained to be entirely toppled. The very insensitive would be scarcely affected—oh, such people as some of our older, work-broken peasants. Well, the children would have fugitive memories, and that, combined with the confused, incoherent babblings of the half-mad morons, formed the basis for the *Book of Revelations*.

"Naturally, the book was based, in the first place, on the testimony of those least qualified to serve as historians; that is, children and morons; and was probably edited and re-edited through the cycles."

"Do you suppose," broke in Theremon, "that they carried the book through the cycles the way we're planning on handing on the secret of gravitation?"

Sheering shrugged. "Perhaps, but their exact method is unimportant. They do it, somehow. The point I was getting at was that the book can't help but be a mass of distortion, even if it is based on fact. For instance, do you remember the experiment with the holes in the roof that Faro and Yimot tried—the one that didn't work?"

"Yes."

"You know why it didn't w——" He stopped and rose in alarm, for Aton was approaching, his face a twisted mask of consternation. "*What's happened?*"

Aton drew him aside and Sheerin could feel the fingers on his elbow twitching.

"Not so loud!" Aton's voice was low and tortured. "I've just gotten word from the Hideout on the private line."

Sheerin broke in anxiously. "They are in trouble?"

"Not *they*." Aton stressed the pronoun significantly. "They sealed themselves off just a while ago, and they're going to stay buried till day after tomorrow. They're safe. But the *city*, Sheerin—it's a shambles. You have no idea——" He was having difficulty in speaking.

"Well?" snapped Sheerin impatiently. "What of it? It will get worse. What are you shaking about?" Then, suspiciously, "How do you feel?"

Aton's eyes sparked angrily at the insinuation, and then

faded to anxiety once more. "You don't understand. The Cultists are active. They're rousing the people to storm the Observatory—promising them immediate entrance into grace, promising them salvation, promising them anything. What are we to do, Sheerin?"

Sheerin's head bent, and he stared in long abstraction at his toes. He tapped his chin with one knuckle, then looked up and said crisply, "Do? What is there to do? Nothing at all. Do the men know of this?"

"No, of course not!"

"Good! Keep it that way. How long till totality?"

"Not quite an hour."

"There's nothing to do but gamble. It will take time to organize any really formidable mob, and it will take more time to get them out here. We're a good five miles from the city—"

He glared out the window, down the slopes to where the farmed patches gave way to clumps of white houses in the suburbs; down to where the metropolis itself was a blur on the horizon—a mist in the waning blaze of Beta.

He repeated without turning, "It will take time. Keep on working and pray that totality comes first."

Beta was cut in half, the line of division pushing a slight concavity into the still-bright portion of the Sun. It was like a gigantic eyelid shutting slantwise over the light of a world.

The faint clatter of the room in which he stood faded into oblivion, and he sensed only the thick silence of the fields outside. The very insects seemed frightened mute. And things were dim.

He jumped at the voice in his ear. Theremon said, "Is something wrong?"

"Eh? Er—no. Get back to the chair. We're in the way." They slipped back to their corner, but the psychologist did not speak for a time. He lifted a finger and loosened his collar. He twisted his neck back and forth but found no relief. He looked up suddenly.

"Are you having any difficulty in breathing?"

The newspaperman opened his eyes wide and drew two or three long breaths. "No. Why?"

"I looked out the window too long, I suppose. The dimness got me. Difficulty in breathing is one of the first symptoms of a claustrophobic attack."

Theremon drew another long breath. "Well, it hasn't got me yet. Say, here's another of the fellows."

Beenay had interposed his bulk between the light and the pair in the corner, and Sheerin squinted up at him anxiously. "Hello, Beenay."

The astronomer shifted his weight to the other foot and smiled feebly. "You won't mind if I sit down awhile and join in the talk? My cameras are set, and there's nothing to do till totality." He paused and eyed the Cultist, who fifteen minutes earlier had drawn a small, skin-bound book from his sleeve and had been poring intently over it ever since. "That rat hasn't been making trouble, has he?"

Sheerin shook his head. His shoulders were thrown back and he frowned his concentration as he forced himself to breathe regularly. He said, "Have you had any trouble breathing, Beenay?"

Beenay sniffed the air in his turn. "It doesn't seem stuffy to me."

"A touch of claustrophobia," explained Sheerin apologetically.

"Ohhh! It worked itself differently with me. I get the impression that my eyes are going back on me. Things seem to blur and—well, nothing is clear. And it's cold, too."

"Oh, it's cold, all right. That's no illusion." Theremon grimaced. "My toes feel as if I've been shipping them cross-country in a refrigerating car."

"What we need," put in Sheerin, "is to keep our minds busy with extraneous affairs. I was telling you a while ago, Theremon, why Faro's experiments with the holes in the roof came to nothing."

"You were just beginning," replied Theremon. He encircled a knee with both arms and nuzzled his chin against it.

"Well, as I started to say, they were misled by taking the *Book of Revelations* literally. There probably wasn't any sense in attaching any physical significance to the Stars. It might be, you know, that in the presence of total Darkness, the mind finds it absolutely necessary to create light. This illusion of light might be all the Stars there really are."

"In other words," interposed Theremon, "you mean the Stars are the results of the madness and not one of the causes. Then, what good will Beenay's photographs be?"

"To prove that it is an illusion, maybe; or to prove the opposite; for all I know. Then again—"

But Beenay had drawn his chair closer, and there was an expression of sudden enthusiasm on his face. "Say, I'm glad you two got onto this subject." His eyes narrowed and he lifted one finger. "I've been thinking about these Stars and I've got a really cute notion. Of course it's strictly ocean foam, and I'm not trying to advance it seriously, but I think it's interesting. Do you want to hear it?"

He seemed half reluctant, but Sheerin leaned back and said, "Go ahead! I'm listening."

"Well, then, supposing there were other suns in the universe." He broke off a little bashfully. "I mean suns that are so far away that they're too dim to see. It sounds as if I've been reading some of that fantastic fiction, I suppose."

"Not necessarily. Still, isn't that possibility eliminated by the fact that, according to the Law of Gravitation, they would make themselves evident by their attractive forces?"

"Not if they were far enough off," rejoined Beenay, "really far off—maybe as much as four light years, or even more. We'd never be able to detect perturbations then, because they'd be too small. Say that there were a lot of suns that far off; a dozen or two, maybe."

Theremon whistled melodiously. "What an idea for a good Sunday supplement article. Two dozen suns in a universe eight light years across. Wow! That would shrink our world into insignificance. The readers would eat it up."

"Only an idea," said Beenay with a grin, "but you see the point. During an eclipse, these dozen suns would become visible because there'd be no *real* sunlight to drown them out. Since they're so far off, they'd appear small, like so many little marbles. Of course the Cultists talk of millions of Stars, but that's probably exaggeration. There just isn't any place in the universe you could put a million suns—unless they touch one another."

Sheerin had listened with gradually increasing interest. "You've hit something there, Beenay. And exaggeration is just exactly what would happen. Our minds, as you probably know, can't grasp directly any number higher than five; above that there is only the concept of 'many.' A dozen would become a million just like that. A damn good idea!"

"And I've got another cute little notion," Beenay said. "Have you ever thought what a simple problem gravitation would be if only you had a sufficiently simple system? Supposing you had a universe in which there was a planet with only one sun. The planet would travel in a perfect ellipse and the exact nature of the gravitational force would be so evident it could be accepted as an axiom. Astronomers on such a world would start off with gravity probably before they even invented the telescope. Naked-eye observation would be enough."

"But would such a system be dynamically stable?" questioned Sheerin doubtfully.

"Sure! They call it the 'one-and-one' case. It's been worked out mathematically, but it's the philosophical implications that interest me."

"It's nice to think about," admitted Sheerin, "as a pretty abstraction—like a perfect gas, or absolute zero."

"Of course," continued Beenay, "there's the catch that life would be impossible on such a planet. It wouldn't get enough heat and light, and if it rotated there would be total Darkness half of each day. You couldn't expect life—which is fundamentally dependent upon light—to develop under those conditions. Besides—"

Sheerin's chair went over backward as he sprang to his feet in a rude interruption. "Aton's brought out the lights."

Beenay said, "Huh," turned to stare, and then grinned halfway around his head in open relief.

There were half a dozen foot-long, inch-thick rods cradled in Aton's arms. He glared over them at the assembled staff members.

"Get back to work, all of you. Sheerin, come here and help me!"

Sheerin trotted to the older man's side and, one by one, in utter silence, the two adjusted the rods in makeshift metal holders suspended from the walls.

With the air of one carrying through the most sacred item of a religious ritual, Sheerin scraped a large, clumsy match into spluttering life and passed it to Aton, who carried the flame to the upper end of one of the rods.

It hesitated there awhile, playing futilely about the tip, until a sudden, crackling flare cast Aton's lined face into yellow highlights. He withdrew the match and a spontaneous cheer rattled the window.

The rod was topped by six inches of wavering flame! Methodically, the other rods were lighted, until six independent fires turned the rear of the room yellow.

The light was dim, dimmer even than the tenuous sunlight. The flames reeled crazily, giving birth to drunken, swaying shadows. The torches smoked devilishly and smelled like a bad day in the kitchen. But they emitted yellow light.

There was something about yellow light, after four hours of somber, dimming Beta. Even Latimer had lifted his eyes from his book and stared in wonder.

Sheerin warmed his hands at the nearest, regardless of the soot that gathered upon them in a fine, gray powder, and muttered ecstatically to himself. "Beautiful! Beautiful! I never realized before what a wonderful color yellow is."

But Theremon regarded the torches suspiciously. He

wrinkled his nose at the rancid odor and said, "What are those things?"

"Wood," said Sheerin shortly.

"Oh, no, they're not. They aren't burning. The top inch is charred and the flame just keeps shooting up out of nothing."

"That's the beauty of it. This is a really efficient artificial-light mechanism. We made a few hundred of them, but most went to the Hideout, of course. You see"—he turned and wiped his blackened hands upon his handkerchief—"you take the pithy core of coarse water reeds, dry them thoroughly, and soak them in animal grease. Then you set fire to it and the grease burns, little by little. These torches will burn for almost half an hour without stopping. Ingenious, isn't it? It was developed by one of our own young men at Saro University."

After the momentary sensation, the dome had quieted. Latimer had carried his chair directly beneath a torch and continued reading, lips moving in the monotonous recital of invocations to the Stars. Beenay had drifted away to his cameras once more, and Theremon seized the opportunity to add to his notes on the article he was going to write for the Saro City *Chronicle* the next day—a procedure he had been following for the last two hours in a perfectly methodical, perfectly conscientious and, as he was well aware, perfectly meaningless fashion.

But, as the gleam of amusement in Sheerin's eyes indicated, careful note-taking occupied his mind with something other than the fact that the sky was gradually turning a horrible deep purple-red, as if it were one gigantic, freshly peeled beet; and so it fulfilled its purpose.

The air grew, somehow, denser. Dusk, like a palpable entity, entered the room, and the dancing circle of yellow light about the torches etched itself into ever-sharper distinction against the gathering grayness beyond. There was the odor of smoke and the presence of little chuckling sounds that the torches made as they burned; the soft pad of one of the men circling the table at which he worked, on hesitant tiptoes; the occasional indrawn breath of someone trying to retain composure in a world that was retreating into the shadow.

It was Theremon who first heard the extraneous noise. It was a vague, unorganized *impression* of sound that would have gone unnoticed but for the dead silence that prevailed within the dome.

The newsman sat upright and replaced his notebook. He held his breath and listened; then, with considerable reluctance, threaded his way between the solarscope and one of Beenay's cameras and stood before the window.

The silence ripped to fragments at his startled shout: "*Sheerin!*"

Work stopped! The psychologist was at his side in a moment. Aton joined him. Even Yimot 70, high in his little lean-back seat at the eyepiece of the gigantic solarscope, paused and looked downward.

Outside, Beta was a mere smoldering splinter, taking one last desperate look at Lagash. The eastern horizon, in the direction of the city, was lost in Darkness, and the road from Saro to the Observatory was a dull-red line bordered on both sides by wooded tracts, the trees of which had somehow lost individuality and merged into a continuous shadowy mass.

But it was the highway itself that held attention, for along it there surged another, and infinitely menacing, shadowy mass.

Aton cried in a cracked voice, "The madmen from the city! They've come!"

"How long to totality?" demanded Sheerin.

"Fifteen minutes, but . . . but they'll be here in five."

"Never mind, keep the men working. We'll hold them off. This place is built like a fortress. Aton, keep an eye on our young Cultist just for luck. Theremon, come with me."

Sheerin was out the door, and Theremon was at his heels. The stairs stretched below them in tight, circular sweeps about the central shaft, fading into a dank and dreary grayness.

The first momentum of their rush had carried them fifty feet down, so that the dim, flickering yellow from the open door of the dome had disappeared and both above and below the same dusky shadow crushed in upon them.

Sheerin paused, and his pudgy hand clutched at his chest. His eyes bulged and his voice was a dry cough. "I can't . . . breathe . . . Go down . . . yourself. Close all doors—"

Theremon took a few downward steps, then turned. "Wait! Can you hold out a minute?" He was panting himself. The air passed in and out his lungs like so much molasses, and there was a little germ of screeching panic in his mind at the thought of making his way into the mysterious Darkness below by himself.

Theremon, after all, was afraid of the dark!

"Stay here," he said. "I'll be back in a second." He dashed upward two steps at a time, heart pounding—not altogether from the exertion—tumbled into the dome and snatched a torch from its holder. It was foul-smelling, and the smoke smarted his eyes almost blind, but he clutched that torch as if he wanted to kiss it for joy, and its flame streamed backward as he hurtled down the stairs again.

Sheerin opened his eyes and moaned as Theremon bent over him. Theremon shook him roughly. "All right, get a hold on yourself. We've got light."

He held the torch at tiptoe height and, propping the tottering psychologist by an elbow, made his way downward in the middle of the protecting circle of illumination.

The offices on the ground floor still possessed what light there was, and Theremon felt the horror about him relax.

"Here," he said brusquely, and passed the torch to Sheerin. "You can hear *them* outside."

And they could. Little scraps of hoarse, wordless shouts.

But Sheerin was right; the Observatory was built like a fortress. Erected in the last century, when the neo-Gavottian style of architecture was at its ugly height, it had been designed for stability and durability rather than for beauty.

The windows were protected by the grillwork of inch-thick iron bars sunk deep into the concrete sills. The walls were solid masonry that an earthquake couldn't have touched, and the main door was a huge oaken slab reinforced with iron. Theremon shot the bolts and they slid shut with a dull clang.

At the other end of the corridor, Sheerin cursed weakly. He pointed to the lock of the back door which had been neatly jimmied into uselessness.

"That must be how Latimer got in," he said.

"Well, don't stand there," cried Theremon impatiently. "Help drag up the furniture—and keep that torch out of my eyes. The smoke's killing me."

He slammed the heavy table up against the door as he spoke, and in two minutes had built a barricade which made up for what it lacked in beauty and symmetry by the sheer inertia of its massiveness.

Somewhere, dimly, far off, they could hear the battering of naked fists upon the door; and the screams and yells from outside had a sort of half reality.

That mob had set off from Saro City with only two things in mind: the attainment of Cultist salvation by the destruction of the Observatory, and a maddening fear that all but paralyzed them. There was no time to think of ground cars, or of weapons, or of leadership, or even of organization. They made for the Observatory on foot and assaulted it with bare hands.

And now that they were there, the last flash of Beta, the last ruby-red drop of flame, flickered feebly over a humanity that had left only stark, universal fear!

Theremon groaned, "Let's get back to the dome!"

In the dome, only Yimot, at the solarscope, had kept his place. The rest were clustered about the cameras, and

Beenay was giving his instructions in a hoarse, strained voice.

"Get it straight, all of you. I'm snapping Beta just before totality and changing the plate. That will leave one of you to each camera. You all know about . . . about times of exposure—"

There was a breathless murmur of agreement.

Beenay passed a hand over his eyes. "Are the torches still burning? Never mind, I see them!" He was leaning hard against the back of a chair. "Now remember, don't . . . don't try to look for good shots. Don't waste time trying to get t-two stars at a time in the scope field. One is enough. And . . . and if you feel yourself going, *get away from the camera.*"

At the door, Sheerin whispered to Theremon, "Take me to Aton. I don't see him."

The newsman did not answer immediately. The vague forms of the astronomers wavered and blurred, and the torches overhead had become only yellow splotches.

"It's dark," he whimpered.

Sheerin held out his hand. "Aton." He stumbled forward. "Aton!"

Theremon stepped after and seized his arm. "Wait, I'll take you." Somehow he made his way across the room. He closed his eyes against the Darkness and his mind against the chaos within it.

No one heard them or paid attention to them. Sheerin stumbled against the wall. "Aton!"

The psychologist felt shaking hands touching him, then withdrawing, and a voice muttering, "Is that you, Sheerin?"

"Aton!" He strove to breathe normally. "Don't worry about the mob. The place will hold them off."

Latimer, the Cultist, rose to his feet, and his face twisted in desperation. His word was pledged, and to break it would mean placing his soul in mortal peril. Yet that word had been forced from him and had not been given freely. The

Stars would come soon! He could not stand by and allow—
And yet his word was pledged.

Beenay's face was dimly flushed as it looked upward at
Beta's last ray, and Latimer, seeing him bend over his
camera, made his decision. His nails cut the flesh of his
palms as he tensed himself.

He staggered crazily as he started his rush. There was
nothing before him but shadows; the very floor beneath his
feet lacked substance. And then someone was upon him and
he went down with clutching fingers at his throat.

He doubled his knee and drove it hard into his assailant.
"Let me up or I'll kill you."

Theremon cried out sharply and muttered through a
blinding haze of pain. "You double-crossing rat!"

The newsman seemed conscious of everything at once.
He heard Beenay croak, "I've got it. At your cameras,
men!" and then there was the strange awareness that the last
thread of sunlight had thinned out and snapped.

Simultaneously he heard one last choking gasp from
Beenay, and a queer little cry from Sheerin, a hysterical
giggle that cut off in a rasp—and a sudden silence, a
strange, deadly silence from outside.

And Latimer had gone limp in his loosening grasp.
Theremon peered into the Cultist's eyes and saw the
blankness of them, staring upward, mirroring the feeble
yellow of the torches. He saw the bubble of froth upon
Latimer's lips and heard the low animal whimper in
Latimer's throat.

With the slow fascination of fear, he lifted himself on one
arm and turned his eyes toward the blood-curdling blackness of the window.

Through it shone the Stars!

Not Earth's feeble thirty-six hundred Stars visible to the
eye; Lagash was in the center of a giant cluster. Thirty
thousand mighty suns shone down in a soul-searing splendor that was more frighteningly cold in its awful indiffer-

ence than the bitter wind that shivered across the cold, horribly bleak world.

Theremon staggered to his feet, his throat constricting him to breathlessness, all the muscles of his body writhing in an intensity of terror and sheer fear beyond bearing. He was going mad and knew it, and somewhere deep inside a bit of sanity was screaming, struggling to fight off the hopeless flood of black terror. It was very horrible to go mad and know that you were going mad—to know that in a little minute you would be here physically and yet all the real essence would be dead and drowned in the black madness. For this was the Dark—the Dark and the Cold and the Doom. The bright walls of the universe were shattered and their awful black fragments were falling down to crush and squeeze and obliterate him.

He jostled someone crawling on hands and knees, but stumbled somehow over him. Hands groping at his tortured throat, he limped toward the flame of the torches that filled all his mad vision.

"Light!" he screamed.

Aton, somewhere, was crying, whimpering horribly like a terribly frightened child. "Stars—all the Stars—we didn't know at all. We didn't know anything. We thought six stars in a universe is something the Stars didn't notice is Darkness forever and ever and ever and the walls are breaking in and we didn't know we couldn't know and anything—"

Someone clawed at the torch, and it fell and snuffed out. In the instant, the awful splendor of the indifferent Stars leaped nearer to them.

On the horizon outside the window, in the direction of Saro City, a crimson glow began growing, strengthening in brightness, that was not the glow of a sun.

The long night had come again.

RUNAROUND

It was one of Gregory Powell's favorite platitudes that nothing was to be gained from excitement, so when Mike Donovan came leaping down the stairs toward him, red hair matted with perspiration, Powell frowned.

"What's wrong?" he said. "Break a fingernail?"

"Yaaaah," snarled Donovan feverishly. "What have you been doing in the sublevels all day?" He took a deep breath and blurted out, "Speedy never returned."

Powell's eyes widened momentarily and he stopped on the stairs; then he recovered and resumed his upward steps. He didn't speak until he reached the head of the flight, and then:

"You sent him after the selenium?"

"Yes."

"And how long has he been out?"

"Five hours now."

Silence! This was a devil of a situation. Here they were, on Mercury exactly twelve hours—and already up to the eyebrows in the worst sort of trouble. Mercury had long been the jinx world of the System, but this was drawing it rather strong—even for a jinx.

Powell said, "Start at the beginning, and let's get this straight."

They were in the radio room now—with its already subtly antiquated equipment, untouched for the ten years previous to their arrival. Even ten years, technologically speaking, meant so much. Compare Speedy with the type of robot they must have had back in 2005. But then, advances in robotics these days were tremendous. Powell touched a still gleaming metal surface gingerly. The air of disuse that touched everything about the room—and the entire Station—was infinitely depressing.

Donovan must have felt it. He began: "I tried to locate him by radio, but it was no go. Radio isn't any good on the Mercury Sunside—not past two miles, anyway. That's one of the reasons the First Expedition failed. And we can't put up the ultrawave equipment for weeks yet—"

"Skip all that. What *did* you get?"

"I located the unorganized body signal in the short wave. It was no good for anything except his position. I kept track of him that way for two hours and plotted the results on the map."

There was a yellowed square of parchment in his hip pocket—a relic of the unsuccessful First Expedition—and he slapped it down on the desk with vicious force, spreading it flat with the palm of his hand. Powell, hands clasped across his chest, watched it at long range.

Donovan's pencil pointed nervously. "The red cross is the selenium pool. You marked it yourself."

"Which one is it?" interrupted Powell. "There were three that MacDougal located for us before he left."

"I sent Speedy to the nearest, naturally. Seventeen miles away. But what difference does that make?" There was tension in his voice. "There are the penciled dots that mark Speedy's position."

And for the first time Powell's artificial aplomb was shaken and his hands shot forward for the map.

"Are *you* serious? This is impossible."

"There it is," growled Donovan.

The little dots that marked the position formed a rough circle about the red cross of the selenium pool. And

Powell's fingers went to his brown mustache, the unfailing signal of anxiety.

Donovan added: "In the two hours I checked on him, he circled that damned pool four times. It seems likely to me that he'll keep that up forever. Do you realize the position we're in?"

Powell looked up shortly, and said nothing. Oh, yes, he realized the position they were in. It worked itself out as simply as a syllogism. The photo-cell banks that alone stood between the full power of Mercury's monstrous sun and themselves were shot to hell. The only thing that could save them was selenium. The only thing that could get the selenium was Speedy. If Speedy didn't come back, no selenium. No selenium, no photo-cell banks. No photo-banks—well, death by slow broiling is one of the more unpleasant ways of being done in.

Donovan rubbed his red mop of hair savagely and expressed himself with bitterness. "We'll be the laughing-stock of the System, Greg. How can everything have gone so wrong so soon? The great team of Powell and Donovan is sent out to Mercury to report on the advisability of reopening the Sunside Mining Station with modern techniques and robots and we ruin everything the first day. A purely routine job, too. We'll never live it down."

"We won't have to, perhaps," replied Powell, quietly. "If we don't do something quickly, living anything down—or even just plain living—will be out of the question."

"Don't be stupid! If you feel funny about it, Greg, I don't. It was criminal, sending us out here with only one robot. And it was *your* bright idea that we could handle the photo-cell banks ourselves."

"Now you're being unfair. It was a mutual decision and you know it. All we needed was a kilogram of selenium, a Stillhead Dielectrode Plate and about three hours' time—and there are pools of pure selenium all over Sunside. MacDougal's spectroreflector spotted three for us in five minutes, didn't it? What the devil! We couldn't have waited for next conjunction."

"Well, what are we going to do? Powell, you've got an idea. I know you have, or you wouldn't be so calm. You're no more a hero than I am. Go on, spill it!"

"We can't go after Speedy ourselves, Mike—not on the Sunside. Even the new insosuits aren't good for more than twenty minutes in direct sunlight. But you know the old saying, 'Set a robot to catch a robot.' Look, Mike, maybe things aren't so bad. We've got six robots down in the sublevels, that we may be able to use, if they work. *If* they work."

There was a glint of sudden hope in Donovan's eyes. "You mean six robots from the First Expedition. Are you sure? They may be subrobotic machines. Ten years is a long time as far as robot-types are concerned, you know.

"No, they're robots. I've spent all day with them and I know. They've got positronic brains: primitive, of course." He placed the map in his pocket. "Let's go down."

The robots were on the lowest sublevel—all six of them surrounded by musty packing cases of uncertain content. They were large, extremely so, and even though they were in a sitting position on the floor, legs straddled out before them, their heads were a good seven feet in the air.

Donovan whistled. "Look at the size of them, will you? The chests must be ten feet around."

"That's because they're supplied with the old McGuffy gears. I've been over the insides—crummiest set you've ever seen."

"Have you powered them yet?"

"No. There wasn't any reason to. I don't think there's anything wrong with them. Even the diaphragm is in reasonable order. They might talk."

He had unscrewed the chest plate of the nearest as he spoke, inserted the two-inch sphere that contained the tiny spark of atomic energy that was a robot's life. There was difficulty in fitting it, but he managed, and then screwed the plate back on again in laborious fashion. The radio controls of more modern models had not been heard of ten years earlier. And then to the other five.

Donovan said uneasily, "They haven't moved."

"No orders to do so," replied Powell, succinctly. He went back to the first in the line and struck him on the chest. "You! Do you hear me?"

The monster's head bent slowly and the eyes fixed themselves on Powell. Then, in a harsh, squawking voice— like that of a medieval phonograph, he grated, "Yes, Master!"

Powell grinned humorlessly at Donovan. "Did you get that? Those were the days of the first talking robots when it looked as if the use of robots on Earth would be banned. The makers were fighting that and they built good, healthy slave complexes into the damned machines."

"It didn't help them," muttered Donovan.

"No, it didn't, but they sure tried." He turned once more to the robot. "Get up!"

The robot towered upward slowly and Donovan's head craned and his puckered lips whistled.

Powell said: "Can you go out upon the surface? In the light?"

There was consideration while the robot's slow brain worked. Then, "Yes, Master."

"Good. Do you know what a mile is?"

Another consideration, and another slow answer. "Yes, Master."

"We will take you up to the surface then, and indicate a direction. You will go about seventeen miles, and somewhere in that general region you will meet another robot, smaller than yourself. You understand so far?"

"Yes, Master."

"You will find this robot and order him to return. If he does not wish to, you are to bring him back by force."

Donovan clutched at Powell's sleeve. "Why not send him for the selenium direct?"

"Because I want Speedy back, nitwit. I want to find out what's wrong with him." And to the robot, "All right, you, follow me."

The robot remained motionless and his voice rumbled: "Pardon, Master, but I cannot. You must mount first." His clumsy arms had come together with a thwack, blunt fingers interlacing.

Powell stared and then pinched at his mustache. "Uh . . . oh!"

Donovan's eyes bulged. "We've got to ride him? Like a horse?"

"I guess that's the idea. I don't know why, though. I can't see—Yes, I do. I told you they were playing up robot-safety in those days. Evidently, they were going to sell the notion of safety by not allowing them to move about, without a mahout on their shoulders all the time. What do we do now?"

"That's what I've been thinking," muttered Donovan. "We can't go out on the surface, with a robot or without. Oh, for the love of Pete"—and he snapped his fingers twice. He grew excited. "Give me that map you've got. I haven't studied it for two hours for nothing. This is a Mining Station. What's wrong with using the tunnels?"

The Mining Station was a black circle on the map, and the light dotted lines that were tunnels stretched out about it in spiderweb fashion.

Donovan studied the list of symbols at the bottom of the map. "Look," he said, "the small black dots are openings to the surface, and here's one maybe three miles away from the selenium pool. There's a number here—you'd think they'd write larger—13a. If the robots know their way around here—"

Powell shot the question and received the dull "Yes, Master," in reply. "Get your insosuit," he said with satisfaction.

It was the first time either had worn the insosuits—which marked one time more than either had expected to upon their arrival the day before—and they tested their limb movements uncomfortably.

The insosuit was far bulkier and far uglier than the regulation spacesuit; but withal considerably lighter, due to the fact that they were entirely nonmetallic in composition. Composed of heat-resistant plastic and chemically treated cork layers, and equipped with a desiccating unit to keep the air bone-dry, the insosuits could withstand the full glare of Mercury's sun for twenty minutes. Five to ten minutes more, as well, without actually killing the occupant.

And still the robot's hands formed the stirrup, nor did he betray the slightest atom of surprise at the grotesque figure into which Powell had been converted.

Powell's radio-harshened voice boomed out: "Are you ready to take us to Exit 13a?"

"Yes, Master."

Good, thought Powell; they might lack radio control but at least they were fitted for radio reception. "Mount one or the other, Mike," he said to Donovan.

He placed a foot in the improvised stirrup and swung upward. He found the seat comfortable; there was the humped back of the robot, evidently shaped for the purpose, a shallow groove along each shoulder for the thighs and two elongated "ears" whose purpose now seemed obvious.

Powell seized the ears and twisted the head. His mount turned ponderously. "Lead on, Macduff." But he did not feel at all lighthearted.

The gigantic robots moved slowly, with mechanical precision, through the doorway that cleared their heads by a scant foot, so that the two men had to duck hurriedly, along a narrow corridor in which their unhurried footsteps boomed monotonously and into the air lock.

The long, airless tunnel that stretched to a pinpoint before them brought home forcefully to Powell the exact magnitude of the task accomplished by the First Expedition, with their crude robots and their start-from-scratch necessities. They might have been a failure, but their failure was a good deal better than the usual run of the System's successes.

The robots plodded onward with a pace that never varied and with footsteps that never lengthened.

Powell said: "Notice that these tunnels are blazing with lights and that the temperature is Earth-normal. It's probably been like this all the ten years that this place has remained empty."

"How's that?"

"Cheap energy; cheapest in the System. Sunpower, you know, and on Mercury's Sunside, sunpower is *something*. That's why the Station was built in the sunlight rather than in the shadow of a mountain. It's really a huge energy converter. The heat is turned into electricity, light, mechanical work and what have you; so that energy is supplied and the Station is cooled in a simultaneous process."

"Look," said Donovan. "This is all very educational, but would you mind changing the subject? It so happens that this conversion of energy that you talk about is carried on by the photo-cell banks mainly—and that is a tender subject with me at the moment."

Powell grunted vaguely, and when Donovan broke the resulting silence, it was to change the subject completely. "Listen, Greg. What the devil's wrong with Speedy, anyway? I can't understand it."

It's not easy to shrug shoulders in an insosuit, but Powell tried it. "I don't know, Mike. You know he's perfectly adapted to a Mercurian environment. Heat doesn't mean anything to him and he's built for the light gravity and the broken ground. He's foolproof—or, at least, he should be."

Silence fell. This time, silence that lasted.

"Master," said the robot, "we are here."

"Eh?" Powell snapped out of a semidrowse. "Well, get us out of here—out to the surface."

They found themselves in a tiny substation, empty, airless, ruined. Donovan had inspected a jagged hole in the upper reaches of one of the walls by the light of his pocket flash.

"Meteorite, do you suppose?" he had asked.

Powell shrugged. "To hell with that. It doesn't matter. Let's get out."

A towering cliff on a black, basaltic rock cut off the sunlight, and the deep night shadow of an airless world surrounded them. Before them, the shadow reached out and ended in a knife-edge abruptness into an all-but-unbearable blaze of white light, that glittered from myriad crystals along a rocky ground.

"Space!" gasped Donovan. "It looks like snow." And it did.

Powell's eyes swept the jagged glitter of Mercury to the horizon and winced at the gorgeous brilliance.

"This must be an unusual area," he said. "The general albedo of Mercury is low and most of the soil is gray pumice. Something like the Moon, you know. Beautiful, isn't it?"

He was thankful for the light filters in their visiplates. Beautiful or not, a look at the sunlight through straight glass would have blinded them inside of half a minute.

Donovan was looking at the spring thermometer on his wrist. "Holy smokes, the temperature is eighty centigrade!"

Powell checked his own and said: "Um-m-m. A little high. Atmosphere, you know."

"On Mercury? Are you nuts?"

"Mercury isn't really airless," explained Powell, in absent-minded fashion. He was adjusting the binocular attachments to his visiplate, and the bloated fingers of the insosuit were clumsy at it. "There is a thin exhalation that clings to its surface—vapors of the more volatile elements and compounds that are heavy enough for Mercurian gravity to retain. You know: selenium, iodine, mercury, gallium, potassium, bismuth, volatile oxides. The vapors sweep into the shadows and condense, giving up heat. It's a sort of gigantic still. In fact, if you use your flash, you'll probably find that the side of the cliff is covered with, say, hoar-sulphur, or maybe quicksilver dew.

"It doesn't matter, though. Our suits can stand a measly eighty indefinitely."

Powell had adjusted the binocular attachments, so that he seemed as eye-stalked as a snail.

Donovan watched tensely. "See anything?"

The other did not answer immediately, and when he did, his voice was anxious and thoughtful. "There's a dark spot on the horizon that might be the selenium pool. It's in the right place. But I don't see Speedy."

Powell clambered upward in an instinctive striving for better view, till he was standing in unsteady fashion upon his robot's shoulders. Legs straddled wide, eyes straining, he said: "I think . . . I think—Yes, it's definitely him. He's coming this way."

Donovan followed the pointing finger. He had no binoculars, but there was a tiny moving dot, black against the blazing brilliance of the crystalline ground.

"I see him," he yelled. "Let's get going!"

Powell had hopped down into a sitting position on the robot again, and his suited hand slapped against the Gargantuan's barrel chest. "Get going!"

"Giddy-ap," yelled Donovan, and thumped his heels, spur fashion.

The robots started off, the regular thudding of their footsteps silent in the airlessness, for the nonmetallic fabric of the insosuits did not transmit sound. There was only a rhythmic vibration just below the border of actual hearing.

"Faster," yelled Donovan. The rhythm did not change.

"No use," cried Powell, in reply. "These junk heaps are only geared to one speed. Do you think they're equipped with selective flexors?"

They had burst through the shadow, and the sunlight came down in a white-hot wash and poured liquidly about them.

Donovan ducked involuntarily. "Wow! Is it imagination or do I feel heat?"

"You'll feel more presently," was the grim reply. "Keep your eye on Speedy."

Robot SPD 13 was near enough to be seen in detail now. His graceful, streamlined body threw out blazing highlights as he loped with easy speed across the broken ground. His name was derived from his serial initials, of course, but it was apt, nevertheless, for the SPD models were among the fastest robots turned out by the United States Robots and Mechanical Men Corporation.

"Hey, Speedy," howled Donovan, and waved a frantic hand.

"Speedy!" shouted Powell. "Come here!"

The distance between the men and the errant robot was being cut down momentarily—more by the efforts of Speedy than the slow plodding of the ten-year-old antique mounts of Donovan and Powell.

They were close enough now to notice that Speedy's gait included a peculiar rolling stagger, a noticeable side-to-side lurch—and then, as Powell waved his hand again and sent maximum juice into his compact head-set radio sender, in preparation for another shout, Speedy looked up and saw them.

Speedy hopped to a halt and remained standing for a moment—with just a tiny, unsteady weave, as though he were swaying in a light wind.

Powell yelled: "All right, Speedy. Come here, boy."

Whereupon Speedy's robot voice sounded in Powell's earphones for the first time.

It said: "Hog dog, let's play games. You catch me and I catch you; no love can cut our knife in two. For I'm Little Buttercup, sweet Little Buttercup. Whoops!" Turning on his heel, he sped off in the direction from which he had come, with a speed and fury that kicked up gouts of baked dust.

And his last words as he receded into the distance were,

"There grew a little flower 'neath a great oak tree," followed by a curious metallic clicking that *might* have been a robotic equivalent of a hiccup.

Donovan said weakly: "Where did he pick up the Gilbert and Sullivan? Say, Greg, he . . . he's drunk or something."

"If you hadn't told me," was the bitter response, "I'd never realize it. Let's get back to the cliff. I'm roasting."

It was Powell who broke the desperate silence. "In the first place," he said, "Speedy isn't drunk—not in the human sense—because he's a robot, and robots don't get drunk. However, there's *something* wrong with him which is the robotic equivalent of drunkenness."

"To me, he's drunk," stated Donovan, emphatically, "and all I know is that he thinks we're playing games. And we're not. It's a matter of life and very gruesome death."

"All right. Don't hurry me. A robot's only a robot. Once we find out what's wrong with him, we can fix it and go on."

"*Once*," said Donovan, sourly.

Powell ignored him. "Speedy is perfectly adapted to normal Mercurian environment. But this region"—and his arm swept wide—"is definitely abnormal. There's our clue. Now where do these crystals come from? They might have formed from a slowly cooling liquid; but where would you get liquid so hot that it would cool in Mercury's sun?"

"Volcanic action," suggested Donovan, instantly, and Powell's body tensed.

"Out of the mouths of sucklings," he said in a small, strange voice, and remained very still for five minutes.

Then, he said, "Listen, Mike, what did you say to Speedy when you sent him after the selenium?"

Donovan was taken aback. "Well damn if—I don't know. I just told him to get it."

"Yes, I know. But how? Try to remember the exact words."

"I said . . . uh . . . I said: 'Speedy, we need some

selenium. You can get it such-and-such a place. Go get it.' That's all. What more did you want me to say?"

"You didn't put any urgency into the order, did you?"

"What for? It was pure routine."

Powell sighed. "Well, it can't be helped now—but we're in a fine fix. He had dismounted from the robot, and was sitting, back against the cliff. Donovan joined him and they linked arms. In the distance, the burning sunlight seemed to wait cat-and-mouse for them, and just next to them, the two giant robots were invisible but for the dull red of their photoelectric eyes that stared down at them, unblinking, unwavering and unconcerned.

Unconcerned! As was all this poisonous Mercury, as large in jinx as it was small in size.

Powell's radio voice was tense in Donovan's ear: "Now, look, let's start with the three fundamental Rules of Robotics—the three rules that are built most deeply into a robot's positronic brain." In the darkness, his gloved fingers ticked off each point.

"We have: One, a robot may not injure a human being, or, through inaction, allow a human being to come to harm."

"Right!"

"Two," continued Powell, "a robot must obey the orders given it by human beings except where such orders would conflict with the First Law."

"Right!"

"And three, a robot must protect its own existence as long as such protection does not conflict with the First or Second Laws."

"Right! Now where are we?"

"Exactly at the explanation. The conflict between the various rules is ironed out by the different positronic potentials in the brain. We'll say that a robot is walking into danger and knows it. The automatic potential that Rule 3 sets up turns him back. But suppose you *order* him to walk into that danger. In that case, Rule 2 sets up a counter-potential higher than the previous one and the robot follows orders at the risk of existence."

"Well, I know that. What about it?"

"Let's take Speedy's case. Speedy is one of the latest models, extremely specialized, and as expensive as a battleship. It's not a thing to be lightly destroyed."

"So?"

"So Rule 3 has been strengthened—that was specifically mentioned, by the way, in the advance notices on the SPD models—so that his allergy to danger is unusually high. At the same time, when you sent him out after the selenium, you gave him his order casually and without special emphasis, so that the Rule 2 potential set-up was rather weak. Now, hold on; I'm just stating facts."

"All right, go ahead. I think I get it."

"You see how it works, don't you? There's some sort of danger centering at the selenium pool. It increases as he approaches, and at a certain distance from it the Rule 3 potential, unusually high to start with, exactly balances the Rule 2 potential, unusually low to start with."

Donovan rose to his feet in excitement. "And it strikes an equilibrium. I see. Rule 3 drives him back and Rule 2 drives him forward—"

"So he follows a circle around the selenium pool, staying on the locus of all points of potential equilibrium. And unless we do something about it, he'll stay on that circle forever, giving us the good old runaround." Then, more thoughtfully: "And that, by the way, is what makes him drunk. At potential equilibrium, half the positronic paths of his brain are out of kilter. I'm not a robot specialist, but that seems obvious. Probably he's lost control of just those parts of his voluntary mechanism that a human drunk has. Ve-e-ery pretty."

"But what's the danger? If we knew what he was running from—"

"*You* suggested it. Volcanic action. Somewhere right above the selenium pool is a seepage of gas from the bowels of Mercury. Sulphur dioxide, carbon dioxide—and carbon monoxide. Lots of it—and at this temperature."

Donovan gulped audibly. "Carbon monoxide plus iron gives the volatile iron carbonyl."

"And a robot," added Powell, "is essentially iron." Then, grimly: "There's nothing like deduction. We've determined everything about our problem but the solution. We can't get the selenium ourselves. It's still too far. We can't send these robot horses, because they can't go themselves, and they can't carry us fast enough to keep us from crisping. And we can't catch Speedy, because the dope thinks we're playing games, and he can run sixty miles to our four."

"If one of us goes," began Donovan, tentatively, "and comes back cooked, there'll still be the other."

"Yes," came the sarcastic reply, "it would be a most tender sacrifice—except that a person would be in no condition to give orders before he ever reaches the pool, and I don't think the robots would ever turn back to the cliff without orders. Figure it out! We're two or three miles from the pool—call it two—the robot travels at four miles an hour; and we can last twenty minutes in our suits. It isn't only the heat, remember. Solar radiation out here in the ultraviolet and below is *poison*."

"Um-m-m," said Donovan, "ten minutes short."

"As good as an eternity. And another thing. In order for Rule 3 potential to have stopped Speedy where it did, there must be an appreciable amount of carbon monoxide in the metal-vapor atmosphere—and there must be an appreciable corrosive action therefore. He's been out hours now—and how do we know when a knee joint, for instance, won't be thrown out of kilter and keel him over. It's not only a question of thinking—we've got to think *fast*!"

Deep, dark, dank, dismal silence!

Donovan broke it, voice trembling in an effort to keep itself emotionless. He said: "As long as we can't increase Rule 2 potential by giving further orders, how about working the other way? If we increase the danger, we increase Rule 3 potential and drive him backward."

Powell's visiplate had turned toward him in a silent question.

"You see," came the cautious explanation, "all we need to do to drive him out of his rut is to increase the concentration of carbon monoxide in his vicinity. Well, back at the Station there's a complete analytical laboratory."

"Naturally," assented Powell. "It's a Mining Station."

"All right. There must be pounds of oxalic acid for calcium precipitations."

"Holy space! Mike, you're a genius."

"So-so," admitted Donovan, modestly. "It's just a case of remembering that oxalic acid on heating decomposes into carbon dioxide, water, and good old carbon monoxide. College chem, you know."

"Hey," he shouted, "can you throw?"

"Master?"

"Never mind." Powell damned the robot's molasses-slow brain. He scrabbled up a jagged brick-size rock. "Take this," he said, "and hit the patch of bluish crystals just across the crooked fissure. You see it?"

Donovan pulled at his shoulder. "Too far, Greg. It's almost half a mile off."

"Quiet," replied Powell. "It's a case of Mercurian gravity and a steel throwing arm. Watch, will you?"

The robot's eyes were measuring the distance with machinely accurate stereoscopy. His arm adjusted itself to the weight of the missile and drew back. In the darkness, the robot's motions went unseen, but there was a sudden thumping sound as he shifted his weight, and seconds later the rock flew blackly into the sunlight. There was no air resistance to slow it down, nor wind to turn it aside—and when it hit the ground it threw up crystals precisely in the center of the "blue patch."

Powell yelled happily and shouted, "Let's go back after the oxalic acid, Mike."

And as they plunged into the ruined substation on the way back to the tunnels, Donovan said grimly: "Speedy's been hanging about on this side of the selenium pool, ever since we chased after him. Did you see him?"

"Yes."

"I guess he wants to play games. Well, we'll play his games!"

They were back hours later, with three-liter jars of the white chemical and a pair of long faces. The photo-cell banks were deteriorating more rapidly than had seemed likely. The two steered their robots into the sunlight and toward the waiting Speedy in silence and with grim purpose.

Speedy galloped slowly toward them. "Here we are again. *Whee*! I've made a little list, the piano organist; all people who eat peppermint and puff it in your face."

"We'll puff something in *your* face," muttered Donovan. "He's limping, Greg."

"I noticed that," came the low, worried response. "The monoxide'll get him yet, if we don't hurry."

They were approaching cautiously now, almost sliding, to refrain from setting off the thoroughly irrational robot. Powell was too far off to tell, of course, but even already he could have sworn the crack-brained Speedy was setting himself for a spring.

"Let her go," he gasped. "Count three! One—two—"

Two steel arms drew back and snapped forward simultaneously and two glass jars whirled forward in towering parallel arcs, gleaming like diamonds in the impossible sun. And in a pair of soundless puffs, they hit the ground behind Speedy in crashes that sent the oxalic acid flying like dust.

In the full heat of Mercury's sun, Powell knew it was fizzing like soda water.

Speedy turned to stare, then backed away from it slowly—and as slowly gathered speed. In fifteen seconds, he was leaping directly toward the two humans in an unsteady canter.

Powell did not get Speedy's words just then, though he heard something that resembled, "Lover's professions when uttered in Hessians."

He turned away. "Back to the cliff, Mike. He's out of the rut and he'll be taking orders now. I'm getting hot."

They jogged toward the shadow at the slow monotonous pace of their mounts, and it was not until they had entered it and felt the sudden coolness settle softly about them that Donovan looked back. *"Greg!"*

Powell looked and almost shrieked. Speedy was moving slowly now—so slowly—and in the *wrong direction*. He was drifting; drifting back into his rut; and he was picking up speed. He looked dreadfully close, and dreadfully unreachable, in the binoculars.

Donovan shouted wildly, "After him!" and thumped his robot into its pace, but Powell called him back.

"You won't catch him, Mike—it's no use." He fidgeted on his robot's shoulders and clenched his fist in tight impotence. "Why the devil do I see these things five seconds after it's all over? Mike, we've wasted hours."

"We need more oxalic acid," declared Donovan stolidly. "The concentration wasn't high enough."

"Seven tons of it wouldn't have been enough—and we haven't the hours to spare to get it, even if it were, with the monoxide chewing him away. Don't you see what it is, Mike?"

And Donovan said flatly, "No."

"We were only establishing new equilibriums. When we create new monoxide and increase Rule 3 potential, he moves backward till he's in balance again—and when the monoxide drifted away, he moved forward, and again there was balance."

Powell's voice sounded thoroughly wretched. "It's the same old runaround. We can push at Rule 2 and pull at Rule 3 and we can't get anywhere—we can only change the

position of balance. We've got to get outside both rules."
And then he pushed his robot closer to Donovan's so that
they were sitting face to face, dim shadows in the darkness,
and he whispered, "Mike!"

"Is it the finish?"—dully. "I suppose we go back to the
Station, wait for the banks to fold, shake hands, take
cyanide, and go out like gentlemen." He laughed shortly.

"Mike," repeated Powell earnestly, "we've got to get
Speedy."

"I know."

"Mike," once more, and Powell hesitated before continu-
ing. "There's always Rule 1. I thought of it—earlier—but
it's desperate."

Donovan looked up and his voice livened. "*We're*
desperate."

"All right. According to Rule 1, a robot can't see a
human come to harm because of his own inaction. Two and
3 can't stand against it. They *can't*, Mike."

"Even when the robot is half cra— Well, he's drunk. You
know he is."

"It's the chances you take."

"Cut it. What are you going to do?"

"I'm going out there now and see what Rule 1 will do. If
it won't break the balance, then what the devil—it's either
now or three-four days from now."

"Hold on, Greg. There are human rules of behavior, too.
You don't go out there just like that. Figure out a lottery,
and give me *my* chance."

"All right. First to get the cube of fourteen goes." And
almost immediately, "Twenty-seven forty-four!"

Donovan felt his robot stagger at a sudden push by
Speedy's mount and then Powell was off into the sunlight. Donovan opened his mouth to shout, and then
clicked it shut. Of course, the damn fool had worked out
the cube of fourteen in advance, and on purpose. Just like
him.

· · ·

The sun was hotter than ever and Powell felt a maddening itch in the small of his back. Imagination, probably, or perhaps hard radiation beginning to tell even through the insosuit.

Speedy was watching him, without a word of Gilbert and Sullivan gibberish as greeting. Thank God for that! But he daren't get too close.

He was three hundred yards away when Speedy began backing, a step at a time, cautiously—and Powell stopped. He jumped from his robot's shoulders and landed on the crystalline ground with a light thump and a flying of jagged fragments.

He proceeded on foot, the ground gritty and slippery to his steps, the low gravity causing him difficulty. The soles of his feet tickled with warmth. He cast one glance over his shoulder at the blackness of the cliff's shadow and realized that he had come too far to return—either by himself or by the help of his antique robot. It was Speedy or nothing now, and the knowledge of that constricted his chest.

Far enough! He stopped.

"Speedy," he called. "Speedy!"

The sleek, modern robot ahead of him hesitated and halted his backward steps, then resumed them.

Powell tried to put a note of pleading into his voice, and found it didn't take much acting. "Speedy, I've got to get back to the shadow or the sun'll get me. It's life or death, Speedy. I need you."

Speedy took one step forward and stopped. He spoke, but at the sound Powell groaned, for it was, "When you're lying awake with a dismal headache and repose is tabooed—" It trailed off there, and Powell took time out for some reason to murmur, "Iolanthe."

It was roasting hot! He caught a movement out of the corner of his eye, and whirled dizzily; then stared in utter astonishment, for the monstrous robot on which he had ridden was moving—moving toward him, and without a rider.

He was talking: "Pardon, Master. I must not move without a Master upon me, but you are in danger."

Of course, Rule 1 potential above everything. But he didn't want that clumsy antique; he wanted Speedy. He walked away and motioned frantically: "I order you to stay away. I *order* you to stop!"

It was quite useless. You could not beat Rule 1 potential. The robot said stupidly, "You are in danger, Master."

Powell looked about him desperately. He couldn't see clearly. His brain was in a heated whirl; his breath scorched when he breathed, and the ground all about him was a shimmering haze.

He called a last time, desperately: "*Speedy!* I'm dying, damn you! Where are you? Speedy, I *need* you."

He was still stumbling backward in a blind effort to get away from the giant robot he didn't want, when he felt steel fingers on his arms, and a worried, apologetic voice of metallic timbre in his ears.

"Holy smokes, boss, what are you doing here? And what am *I* doing—I'm so confused—"

"Never mind," murmured Powell, weakly. "Get me to the shadows of the cliff—and hurry!" There was one last feeling of being lifted into the air and a sensation of rapid motion and burning heat, and he passed out.

He woke with Donovan bending over him and smiling anxiously. "How are you, Greg?"

"Fine!" came the response. "Where's Speedy?"

"Right here. I sent him out to one of the other selenium pools—with orders to get that selenium at all cost this time. He got it back in forty-two minutes and three seconds. I timed him. He still hasn't finished apologizing for the runaround he gave us. He's scared to come near you for fear of what you'll say."

"Drag him over," ordered Powell. "It wasn't his fault."

He held out a hand and gripped Speedy's metal paw. "It's O.K., Speedy." Then, to Donovan, "You know, Mike, I was just thinking—"

"Yes?"

"Well,"—he rubbed his face—the air was so delightfully cool, "you know that when we get things set up here and Speedy put through his Field Tests, they're going to send us to the Space Station next—"

"No!"

"Yes! At least that's what old lady Calvin told me just before we left, and I didn't say anything about it, because I was going to fight the whole idea."

"Fight it?" cried Donovan. "But—"

"I know. It's all right with me now. Two hundred seventy-three degrees Centigrade below zero. Won't it be a pleasure?"

"Space Station," said Donovan, "here I come."

DEATH SENTENCE

Brand Gorla smiled uncomfortably, "These things exaggerate, you know."

"No, no, no!" The little man's albino-pink eyes snapped. "Dorlis was great when no human had ever entered the Vegan System. It was the capital of a Galactic Confederation greater than ours."

"Well, then, let's say that it was an ancient capital. I'll admit that and leave the rest to an archaeologist."

"Archaeologists are no use. What I've discovered needs a specialist in its own field. And you're on the Board."

Brand Gorla looked doubtful. He remembered Theor Realo in senior year—a little white misfit of a human who skulked somewhere in the background of his reminiscences. It had been a long time ago, but the albino had been queer. *That* was easy to remember. And he was still queer.

"I'll try to help," Brand said, "if you'll tell me what you want."

Theor watched intently, "I want you to place certain facts before the Board. Will you promise that?"

Brand hedged, "Even if I help you along, Theor, I'll have to remind you that I'm junior member of the Psychological Board. I haven't much influence."

"You must do your best. The facts will speak for themselves." The albino's hands were trembling.

"Go ahead." Brand resigned himself. The man was an

109

old school fellow. You couldn't be *too* arbitrary about things.

Brand Gorla leaned back and relaxed. The light of Arcturus shone through the ceiling-high windows, diffused and mellowed by the polarizing glass. Even this diluted version of sunlight was too much for the pink eyes of the other, and he shaded his eyes as he spoke.

"I've lived on Dorlis twenty-five years, Brand," he said. "I've poked into places no one today knew existed, and I've found things. Dorlis was the scientific and cultural capital of a civilization greater than ours. Yes it was, and particularly in psychology."

"Things in the past always seem greater." Brand condescended a smile. "There is a theorem to that effect which you'll find in any elementary text. Freshmen invariably call it the 'GOD Theorem.' Stands for 'Good-Old-Days,' you know. But go on."

Theor frowned at the digression. He hid the beginning of a sneer, "You can always dismiss an uncomfortable fact by pinning a dowdy label to it. But tell me this. What do you know of Psychological Engineering?"

Brand shrugged, "No such thing. Anyway, not in the strict mathematical sense. All propaganda and advertising is a crude form of hit-and-miss Psych Engineering—and pretty effective sometimes. Maybe that's what you mean."

"Not at all. I mean actual experimentation, with masses of people, under controlled conditions, and over a period of years."

"Such things have been discussed. It's not feasible in practice. Our social structure couldn't stand much of it, and we don't know enough to set up effective controls."

Theor suppressed excitement, "But the ancients *did* know enough. And they *did* set up controls."

Brand considered phlegmatically, "Startling and interesting, but how do you know?"

"Because I found the documents relating to it." He paused breathlessly. "An entire planet, Brand. A complete world picked to suit, peopled with beings under strict control from every angle. Studied, and charted, and experimented upon. Don't you get the picture?"

Brand noted none of the usual stigmata of mental control. A closer investigation, perhaps—

He said evenly, "You must have been misled. It's thoroughly impossible. You can't control humans like that. Too many variables."

"And that's the point, Brand. They weren't humans."

"What?"

"They were robots, positronic robots. A whole world of them, Brand, with nothing to do but live and react and be observed by a set of psychologists that were *real* psychologists."

"That's mad!"

"I have proof—because that robot world still exists. The First Confederation went to pieces, but that robot world kept on going. It still exists."

"And how do you know?"

Theor Realo stood up. "Because I've been there these last twenty-five years!"

The Board Master threw his formal red-edged gown aside and reached into a pocket for a long, gnarled and decidedly unofficial cigar.

"Preposterous," he grunted, "and thoroughly insane."

"Exactly," said Brand, "and I can't spring it on the Board just like that. They wouldn't listen. I've got to get this across to you first, and then, if you can put your authority behind it—"

"Oh, nuts! I never heard anything as— Who is the fellow?"

Brand sighed, "A crank, I'll admit that. He was in my class at Arcturus U. and a crack-pot albino even then. Maladjusted as the devil, hipped on ancient history, and just the kind that gets an idea and goes through with it by plain, dumb plugging. He's poked about in Dorlis for twenty-five years, he says. He's got the complete records of practically an entire civilization."

The Board Master puffed furiously. "Yeah, I know. In the telestat serials, the brilliant amateur always uncovers the great things. The free lance. The lone wolf. Nuts! Have you consulted the Department of Archaeology?"

"Certainly. And the result was interesting. No one bothers with Dorlis. This isn't just ancient history, you see. It's a matter of fifteen thousand years. It's practically myth. Reputable archaeologists don't waste too much time with it. It's just the thing a book-struck layman with a single-track mind *would* uncover. After this, of course, if the business turns out right, Dorlis will become an archaeologist's paradise."

The Board Master screwed his homely face into an appalling grimace. "It's very unflattering to the ego. If there's any truth in all this, the so-called First Confederation must have had a grasp of psychology so far past ours, as to make us out to be blithering imbeciles. Too, they'd have to build positronic robots that would be about seventy-five orders of magnitude above anything we've even blue-printed. Galaxy! Think of the mathematics involved."

"Look, sir, I've consulted just about everybody. I wouldn't bring this thing to you if I weren't certain that I had every angle checked. I went to Blak just about the first thing, and he's consultant mathematician to United Robots. He says there's no limit to these things. Given the time, the money, and the *advance in psychology*—get that—robots like that could be built right now."

"What proof has he?"

"Who, Blak?"

"No, no! Your friend. The albino. You said he had papers."

"He has. I've got them here. He's got documents—and there's no denying their antiquity. I've had that checked every way from Sunday. I can't read them, of course. I don't know if anyone can, except Theor Realo."

"That's stacking the deck, isn't it? We have to take his say-so."

"Yes, in a way. But he doesn't claim to be able to decipher more than portions. He says it is related to ancient Centaurian, and I've put linguists to work on it. It can be cracked and if his translation isn't accurate, we'll know about it."

"All right. Let's see it."

Brand Gorla brought out the plastic-mounted documents. The Board Master tossed them aside and reached for the translation. Smoke billowed as he read.

"Humph," was his comment. "Further details are on Dorlis, I suppose."

"Theor claims that there are some hundred to two hundred tons of blueprints altogether, on the brain plan of the positronic robots alone. They're still there in the original vault. But that's the least of it. He's been on the robot world itself. He's got photocasts, teletype recordings, all sorts of details. They're not integrated, and obviously the work of a layman who knows next to nothing about psychology. Even so, he's managed to get enough data to prove pretty conclusively that the world he was on wasn't . . . uh . . . natural."

"You've got that with you, too."

"All of it. Most of it's on microfilm, but I've brought the projector. Here are your eyepieces."

An hour later, the Board Master said, "I'll call a Board Meeting tomorrow and push this through."

Brand Gorla grinned tightly, "We'll send a commission to Dorlis?"

"When," said the Board Master dryly, "and if we can get an appropriation out of the University for such an affair. Leave this material with me for the while, please. I want to study it a little more."

Theoretically, the Governmental Department of Science and Technology exercises administrative control over all scientific investigation. Actually, however, the pure research groups of the large universities are thoroughly autonomous bodies, and, as a general rule, the Government does not care to dispute that. But a general rule is not necessarily a universal rule.

And so, although the Board Master scowled and fumed and swore, there was no way of refusing Wynne Murry an interview. To give Murry his complete title, he was under secretary in charge of psychology, psychopathy and mental technology. And he was a pretty fair psychologist in his own right.

So the Board Master might glare, but that was all.

Secretary Murry ignored the glare cheerfully. He rubbed his long chin against the grain and said, "It amounts to a case of insufficient information. Shall we put it that way?"

The Board Master said frigidly, "I don't see what information you want. The government's say in university appropriations is purely advisory, and in this case, I might say, the advice is unwelcome."

Murry shrugged, "I have no quarrel with the appropriation. But you're not going to leave the planet without government permit. That's where the insufficient information comes in."

"There is no information other than we've given you."

"But things have leaked out. All this is childish and rather unnecessary secrecy."

The old psychologist flushed. "Secrecy! If you don't know the academic way of life, I can't help you. Investigations, especially those of major importance, aren't, and can't be, made public, until definite progress has been made. When we get back, we'll send you copies of whatever papers we publish."

Murry shook his head, "Uh-uh. Not enough. You're going to Dorlis, aren't you?"

"We've informed the Department of Science of that."

"Why?"

"Why do you want to know?"

"Because it's big, or the Board Master wouldn't go himself. What's this about an older civilization and a world of robots?"

"Well, then, you know."

"Only vague notions we've been able to scrabble up. I want the details."

"There are none that we know now. We won't know until we're on Dorlis."

"Then I'm going with you."

"What?"

"You see, I want the details, too."

"Why?"

"Ah," Murry unfolded his legs and stood up, "now *you're* asking the questions. It's no use, now. I know that the universities aren't keen on government supervision; and I know that I can expect no willing help from *any* academic source. But, by Arcturus, I'm going to get help this time, and I don't care how you fight it. Your expedition is going nowhere, unless I go with you—representing the government."

Dorlis, as a world, is not impressive. Its importance to Galactic economy is nil, its position far off the great trade routes, its natives backward and unenlightened, its history obscure. And yet somewhere in the heaps of rubble that clutter an ancient world, there is obscure evidence of an influx of flame and destruction that destroyed the Dorlis of an earlier day—the greater capital of a greater Federation.

And somewhere in that rubble, men of a newer world poked and probed and tried to understand.

The Board Master shook his head and then pushed back his grizzling hair. He hadn't shaved in a week.

"The trouble is," he said, "that we have no point of reference. The language can be broken, I suppose, but nothing can be done with the notation."

"I think a great deal has been done."

"Stabs in the dark! Guessing games based on the translations of your albino friend. I won't base any hopes on that."

Brand said, "Nuts! You spent two years on the Nimiam Anomaly, and so far only two months on this, which happens to be a hundred thousand times the job. It's something else that's getting you." He smiled grimly. "It doesn't take a psychologist to see that the government man is in your hair."

The Board Master bit the end off a cigar and spat it four feet. He said slowly, "There are three things about the mule-headed idiot that make me sore. First, I don't like government interference. Second, I don't like a stranger sniffing about when we're on top of the biggest thing in the history of psychology. Third, what in the Galaxy does he want? *What is he after*?"

"I don't know."

"What *should* he be after? Have you thought of it at all?"

"No. Frankly, I don't care. I'd ignore him if I were you."

"You would," said the Board Master violently. "You would! You think the government's entrance into this affair need only be ignored. I suppose you know that this Murry calls himself a psychologist?"

"I know that."

"And I suppose you know he's been displaying a devouring interest in all that we've been doing."

"That, I should say, would be natural."

"Oh! And you know further—" His voice dropped with startling suddenness. "All right, Murry's at the door. Take it easy."

Wynne Murry grinned a greeting, but the Board Master nodded unsmilingly.

"Well, sir," said Murry bluffly, "do you know I've been on my feet for forty-eight hours? You've *got* something here. Something big."

"Thank you."

"No, no. I'm serious. The robot world exists."

"Did you think it didn't?"

The secretary shrugged amiably. "One has a certain natural skepticism. What are your future plans?"

"Why do you ask?" The Board Master grunted his words as if they were being squeezed out singly.

"To see if they jibe with my own."

"And what are your own?"

The secretary smiled. "No, no. You take precedence. How long do you intend staying here?"

"As long as it takes to make a fair beginning on the documents involved."

"That's no answer. What do you mean by a fair beginning?"

"I haven't the slightest idea. It might take years."

"Oh, damnation."

The Board Master raised his eyebrows and said nothing.

The secretary looked at his nails. "I take it you know the location of this robot world."

"Naturally. Theor Realo was there. His information up to now has proven very accurate."

"That's right. The albino. Well, why not go there?"

"Go there! Impossible!"

"May I ask why?"

"Look," said the Board Master with restrained impatience, "you're not here by our invitation, and we're not asking you to dictate our course of actions, but just to show you that I'm not looking for a fight, I'll give you a little metaphorical treatment of our case. Suppose we were presented with a huge and complicated machine, composed of principles and materials of which we knew next to nothing. It is so vast we can't even make out the relationship of the parts, let alone the purpose of the whole. Now, would you advise me to begin attacking the delicate mysterious moving parts of the machine with a detonating ray before I know what it's all about?"

"I see your point, of course, but you're becoming a mystic. The metaphor is farfetched."

"Not at all. These positronic robots were constructed

along lines we know nothing of as yet and were intended to follow lines with which we are entirely unacquainted. About the only thing we know is that the robots were put aside in complete isolation, to work out their destiny by themselves. To ruin that isolation would be to ruin the experiment. If we go there in a body, introducing new, unforeseen factors, inducing unintended reactions, everything is ruined. The littlest disturbance—"

"Poppycock! Theor Realo has already gone there."

The Board Master lost his temper suddenly. "Don't you suppose I know that? Do you suppose it would ever have happened if that cursed albino hadn't been an ignorant fanatic without any knowledge of psychology at all? Galaxy knows what the idiot has done in the way of damage."

There was a silence. The secretary clicked his teeth with a thoughtful fingernail. "I don't know . . . I don't know. But I've got to find out. And I can't wait years."

He left, and the Board Master turned seethingly to Brand, "And how are we going to stop him from going to the robot world if he wants to?"

"I don't see how he can go if we don't let him. *He* doesn't head the expedition."

"Oh, doesn't he? *That's* what I was about to tell you just before he came in. Ten ships of the fleet have landed on Dorlis since we arrived."

"*What!*"

"Just that."

"But what for?"

"That, my boy, is what I don't understand, either."

"Mind if I drop in?" said Wynne Murry, pleasantly, and Theor Realo looked up in sudden anxiety from the papers that lay in hopeless disarray on the desk before him.

"Come in. I'll clear off a seat for you." The albino hustled the mess off one of the two chairs in a state of twittering nerves.

Murry sat down and swung one long leg over the other.

"Are you assigned a job here, too?" He nodded at the desk.

Theor shook his head and smiled feebly. Almost automatically, he brushed the papers together in a heap and turned them face down.

In the months since he had returned to Dorlis with a hundred psychologists of various degrees of renown, he felt himself pushed farther and farther from the center of things. There was room for him no longer. Except to answer questions on the actual state of things upon the robot world, which he alone had visited, he played no part. And even there he detected, or seemed to detect, anger that *he* should have gone, and not a competent scientist.

It was a thing to be resented. Yet, somehow, it had always been like that.

"Pardon me?" He had let Murry's next remark slip.

The secretary repeated, "I say it's surprising you're *not* put to work, then. You made the original discovery, didn't you?"

"Yes," the albino brightened. "But it went out of my hands. It got beyond me."

"You were on the robot world, though."

"That was a mistake, they tell me. I might have ruined everything."

Murry grimaced. "What really gets them, I guess, is that you've got a lot of firsthand dope they didn't. Don't let their fancy titles fool you into thinking you're a nobody. You and I—I'm a layman, too, you know—have to stand up for our rights. Here, have a cigarette."

"I don't sm— I'll take one, thank you." The albino felt himself warming to the long-bodied man opposite. He turned the papers face upward again, and lit up, bravely but uncertainly.

"Twenty-five years." Theor spoke carefully, skirting around urgent coughs.

"Would you answer a few questions about the world?"

"I suppose so. That's all they ever ask me about. But hadn't you better ask *them*? They've probably got it all worked out now." He blew the smoke as far from himself as possible.

Murry said, "Frankly, they haven't even begun, and I want the information without benefit of confusing psychological translation. First of all, what kind of people—or things—are these robots? You haven't a photocast of one of them, have you?"

"Well, no. I didn't like to take 'casts of them. But they're not things. They're *people!*"

"No? Do they look like—people?"

"Yes—mostly. Outside, anyway. I brought some microscopic studies of the cellular structure that I got hold of. The Board Master has them. They're different inside, you know, greatly simplified. But you'd never know that. They're interesting—and nice."

"Are they simpler than the other life on the planet?"

"Oh, no. It's a very primitive planet. And . . . and," he was interrupted by a spasm of coughing and crushed the cigarette to death as unobtrusively as possible. "They've got a protoplasmic base, you know. I don't think they have the slightest idea they're robots."

"No. I don't suppose they would have. What about their science?"

"I don't know. I never got a chance to see. And everything was so different. I guess it would take an expert to understand."

"Did they have machines?"

The albino looked surprised. "Well, of course. A good many, of all sorts."

"Large cities?"

"Yes!"

The secretary's eyes grew thoughtful. "And you like them. Why?"

Theor Realo was brought up sharply. "I don't know. They were just likable. We got along. They didn't bother me so. It's nothing I can put my finger on. Maybe it's because I have it so hard getting along back home, and they weren't as difficult as real people."

"They were more friendly?"

"N-no. Can't say so. They never quite accepted me. I was a stranger, didn't know their language at first—all that. But"—he looked up with sudden brightness—"I understood them better. I could tell what they were thinking better. I— But I don't know why."

"Hm-m-m. Well—another cigarette? No? I've got to be walloping the pillow now. It's getting late. How about a twosome at golf tomorrow? I've worked up a little course. It'll do. Come on out. The exercise will put hair on your chest."

He grinned and left.

He mumbled one sentence to himself: "It looks like a death sentence"—and whistled thoughtfully as he passed along to his own quarters.

He repeated the phrase to himself when he faced the Board Master the next day, with the sash of office about his waist. He did not sit down.

"Again?" said the Board Master, wearily.

"Again!" assented the secretary. "But real business this time. I may have to take over direction of your expedition."

"What! Impossible, sir! I will listen to no such proposition."

"I have my authority." Wynne Murry presented the metalloid cylinder that snapped open at a flick of the thumb. "I have full powers and full discretion as to their use. It is signed, as you will observe, by the chairman of the Congress of the Federation."

"So— But why?" The Board Master, by an effort, breathed normally. "Short of arbitrary tyranny, is there a reason?"

"A very good one, sir. All along, we have viewed this expedition from different angles. The Department of Science and Technology views the robot world not from the

point of view of a scientific curiosity, but from the standpoint of its interference with the peace of the Federation. I
don't think you've ever stopped to consider the danger
inherent in this robot world."

"None that I can see. It is thoroughly isolated and
thoroughly harmless."

"How can you know?"

"From the very nature of the experiment," shouted the
Board Master angrily. "The original planners wanted as
nearly a completely closed system as possible. Here they
are, just as far off the trade routes as possible, in a thinly
populated region of space. The whole idea was to have the
robots develop free of interference."

Murry smiled. "I disagree with you there. Look, the
whole trouble with you is that you're a theoretical man. You
look at things the way they ought to be and I, a practical
man, look at things as they are. No experiment can be set up
and allowed to run indefinitely under its own power. It is
taken for granted that somewhere there is at least an
observer who watches and *modifies* as circumstances
warrant."

"Well?" said the Board Master stolidly.

"Well, the observers in this experiment, the original
psychologists of Dorlis, passed away with the First Confederation, and for fifteen thousand years the experiment
has proceeded by itself. Little errors have added up and
become big ones and introduced alien factors which induced
still other errors. It's a geometric progression. And there's
been no one to halt it."

"Pure hypothesis."

"Maybe. But you're interested only in the robot world,
and I've got to think of the entire Federation."

"And just what possible danger can the robot world be to
the Federation? I don't know *what* in Arcturus you're
driving at, man."

Murry sighed. "I'll be simple, but don't blame me if I
sound melodramatic. The Federation hasn't had any internal

warfare for centuries. What will happen if we come into contact with these robots?"

"Are you afraid of one world?"

"Could be. What about their science? Robots can do funny things sometimes."

"What science can they have? They're not metal-electricity supermen. They're weak protoplasmic creatures, a poor imitation of actual humanity, built around a positronic brain adjusted to a set of simplified human psychological laws. If the word 'robot' is scaring you—"

"No, it isn't, but I've talked to Theor Realo. He's the only one who's seen them, you know."

The Board Master cursed silently and fluently. It came of letting a weak-minded freak of a layman get underfoot where he could babble and do harm.

He said, "We've got Realo's full story, and we've evaluated it fully and capably. I assure you, no harm exists in them. The experiment is so thoroughly academic, I wouldn't spend two days on it if it weren't for the broad scope of the thing. From what we see, the whole idea was to build up a positronic brain containing modifications of one or two of the fundamental axioms. We haven't worked out the details, but they must be minor, as it was the first experiment of this nature ever tried, and even the great mythical psychologists of that day had to progress stepwise. Those robots, I tell you, are neither supermen nor beasts. I assure you—as a psychologist."

"Sorry! I'm a psychologist, too. A little more rule-of-thumb, I'm afraid. That's all. But even little modifications! Take the general spirit of combativeness. That isn't the scientific term, but I've no patience for that. You know what I mean. We humans used to be combative. But it's being bred out of us. A stable political and economic system doesn't encourage the waste energy of combat. It's not a survival factor. But suppose the robots are combative. Suppose as the result of a wrong turn during the millennia they've been unwatched, they've become far more combative than ever their first makers intended. They'd be uncomfortable things to be with."

"And suppose all the stars in the Galaxy became novae at the same time. Let's *really* start worrying."

"And there's another point." Murry ignored the other's heavy sarcasm. "Theor Realo liked those robots. He liked robots better than he likes real people. He felt that he fitted there, and we all know he's been a bad misfit in his own world."

"And what," asked the Board Master, "is the significance of that?"

"You don't see it?" Wynne Murry lifted his eyebrows. "Theor Realo likes those robots because he is *like* them, obviously. I'll guarantee right now that a complete psychic analysis of Theor Realo will show a modification of several fundamental axioms, and the same ones as in the robots.

"And," the secretary drove on without a pause, "Theor Realo worked for a quarter of a century to prove a point, when all science would have laughed him to death if they had known about it. There's fanaticism there; good, honest, *inhuman* perseverance. *Those robots are probably like that!*"

"You're advancing no logic. You're arguing like a maniac, like a moon-struck idiot."

"I don't need strict mathematical proof. Reasonable doubt is sufficient. I've got to protect the Federation. Look, it is reasonable, you know. The psychologists of Dorlis weren't as super as all that. They had to advance stepwise, as you yourself pointed out. Their humanoids—let's not call them robots—were only imitations of human beings and they couldn't be good ones. Humans possess certain very, *very* complicated reaction systems—things like social consciousness, and a tendency toward the establishment of ethical systems; and more ordinary things like chivalry, generosity, fair play and so on, that simply can't possibly be duplicated. I don't think those humanoids can have them.

But they *must* have perseverance, which practically implies stubbornness and combativeness, if my notion on Theor Realo holds good. Well, if their science is anywhere at all, then I don't want to have them running loose in the Galaxy, if our numbers are a thousand or million times theirs. And I don't intend to permit them to do so!"

The Board Master's face was rigid. "What are your immediate intentions?"

"As yet undecided. But I think I am going to organize a small-scale landing on the planet."

"Now, wait." The old psychologist was up and around the desk. He seized the secretary's elbow. "Are you quite certain you know what you're doing? The potentialities in this massive experiment are beyond any possible precalculation by you or me. You can't know what you're destroying."

"I know. Do you think I enjoy what I'm doing? This isn't a hero's job. I'm enough of a psychologist to want to know what's going on, but I've been sent here to protect the Federation, and to the best of my ability I intend doing it—and a dirty job it is. But I can't help it."

"You can't have thought it out. What can you know of the insight it will give us into the basic ideas of psychology? This will amount to a fusion of two Galactic systems, that will send us to heights that will make up in knowledge and power a million times the amount of harm the robots could ever do, if they *were* metal-electricity supermen."

The secretary shrugged. "Now you're the one that is playing with faint possibilities."

"Listen, I'll make a deal. Blockade them. Isolate them with your ships. Mount guards. But don't touch them. Give us more time. Give us a chance. You must!"

"I've thought of that. But I would have to get Congress to agree to that. It would be expensive, you know."

The Board Master flung himself into his chair in wild impatience. "What kind of expense are you talking about? Do you realize the nature of the repayment if we succeed?"

Murry considered; then, with a half smile, "What if they develop interstellar travel?"

The Board Master said quickly, "Then I'll withdraw my objections."

The secretary rose, "I'll have it out with Congress."

Brand Gorla's face was carefully emotionless as he watched the Board Master's stooped back. The cheerful pep talks to the available members of the expedition lacked meat, and he listened to them impatiently.

He said, "What are we going to do now?"

The Board Master's shoulders twitched and he didn't turn. "I've sent for Theor Realo. That little fool left for the Eastern Continent last week—"

"Why?"

The older man blazed at the interruption. "How can I understand anything that freak does! Don't you see that Murry's right? He's a psychic abnormality. We had no business leaving him unwatched. If I had ever thought of looking at him twice, I wouldn't have. He's coming back now, though, and he's going to stay back." His voice fell to a mumble. "Should have been back two hours ago."

"It's an impossible position, sir," said Brand, flatly.

"Think so?"

"Well— Do *you* think Congress will stand for an indefinite patrol off the robot world? It runs into money, and average Galactic citizens aren't going to see it as worth the taxes. The psychological equations degenerate into the axioms of common sense. In fact, I don't see why Murry agreed to consult Congress."

"Don't you?" The Board Master finally faced his junior. "Well, the fool considers himself a psychologist, Galaxy help us, and that's his weak point. He flatters himself that he doesn't want to destroy the robot world in his heart, but that it's the good of the Federation that requires it. And he'll jump at any reasonable compromise. Congress won't agree to it indefinitely, you don't have to point that out to me." He was talking quietly, patiently. "But I will ask for ten years, two years, six months—as much as I can get. I'll get something. In that time, we'll learn new facts about the world. Somehow we'll strengthen our case and renew the agreement when it expires. We'll save the project yet."

There was a short silence and the Board Master added slowly and bitterly, "And that's where Theor Realo plays a vital part."

Brand Gorla watched silently, and waited. The Board Master said, "On that one point, Murry saw what we didn't. Realo is a psychological cripple, and is our real clue to the whole affair. If we study him, we'll have a rough picture of what the robot is like, distorted of course, since his environment had been a hostile, unfriendly one. But we can make allowance for that, estimate his nature in a— Ahh, I'm tired of the whole subject."

The signal box flashed, and the Board Master sighed. "Well, he's here. All right, Gorla, sit down, you make me nervous. Let's take a look at him."

Theor Realo came through the door like a comet and brought himself to a panting halt in the middle of the floor. He looked from one to the other with weak, peering eyes.

"How did all this happen?"

"All what?" said the Board Master coldly. "Sit down. I want to ask you some questions."

"No. You first answer *me*."

"*Sit down!*"

Realo sat. His eyes were brimming. "They're going to destroy the robot world."

"Don't worry about that."

"But you said they could if the robots discovered interstellar travel. You said so. You fool. Don't you see—" He was choking.

The Board Master frowned uneasily. "Will you calm down and talk sense?"

The albino gritted his teeth and forced the words out. "But they'll *have* interstellar travel before long."

And the two psychologists shot toward the little man. "What!!"

"Well . . . well, what do you think?" Realo sprang upward with all the fury of desperation. "Did you think I landed in a desert or in the middle of an ocean and explored a world all by myself? Do you think life is a storybook? I was captured as soon as I landed and taken to a big city. At least, I think it was a big city. It was different from our kind. It had— But I won't tell you."

"Never mind the city," shrieked the Board Master. "You were captured. Go ahead."

"They studied *me*. They studied my machine. And then, one night, I left, to tell the Federation. They didn't know I left. They didn't want me to leave." His voice broke. "And I would have stayed as soon as not, but the Federation had to know."

"Did you tell them anything about your ship?"

"How could I? I'm no mechanic. I don't know the theory or construction. But I showed them how to work the controls and let them look at the motors. That's all."

Brand Gorla said, to himself mostly, "Then they'll never get it. That isn't enough."

The albino's voice raised itself in sudden shrieking triumph. "Oh, yes, they will. I know them. They're machines, you know. They'll work on that problem. And they'll work. And they'll work. And they'll never quit. And they'll get it. They got enough out of me. I'll *bet* they got enough."

The Board Master looked long, and turned away— wearily. "Why didn't you tell us?"

"Because you took my world away from me. I discovered it—by myself—all by myself. And after I had done all the real work, and invited you in, you threw me out. All you had for me was complaints that I had landed on the world and might have ruined everything by interference. Why should I tell you? Find out for yourselves if you're so wise, that you could afford to kick me around."

The Board Master thought bitterly, "Misfit! Inferiority complex! Persecution mania! Nice! It all fits in, now that we've bothered to take our eyes off the horizon and see what was under our nose. And now it's all ruined."

He said, "All right, Realo, we lose. Go away."

Brand Gorla said tightly, "All over? Really all over?"

The Board Master answered, "Really all over. The original experiment, as such, is over. The distortions created by Realo's visit will easily be large enough to make the plans we are studying here a dead language. And besides—Murry is right. If they have interstellar travel, they're dangerous."

Realo was shouting, "But you're not going to destroy them. You can't destroy them. They haven't hurt anyone."

There was no answer, and he raved on, "I'm going back. I'll warn them. They'll be prepared. I'll warn them."

He was backing toward the door, his thin, white hair bristling, his red-rimmed eyes bulging.

The Board Master did not move to stop him when he dashed out.

"Let him go. It was *his* lifetime. I don't care any more."

Theor Realo smashed toward the robot world at an acceleration that was half choking him.

Somewhere ahead was the dustspeck of an isolated world with artificial imitations of humanity struggling along in an experiment that had died. Struggling blindly toward a new goal of interstellar travel that was to be their death sentence.

He was heading toward that world, toward the same city in which he had been "studied" the first time. He remembered it well. Its name was the first words of their language he had learned.

New York!

CATCH THAT RABBIT

The vacation was longer than two weeks. That, Mike Donovan had to admit. It had been six months, with pay. He admitted that, too. But that, as he explained furiously, was fortuitous. U.S. Robots had to get the bugs out of the multiple robot, and there were plenty of bugs, and there are always at least half a dozen bugs left for the field-testing. So they waited and relaxed until the drawing-board men and the slide-rule boys had said "OK!" And now he and Powell were out on the asteroid and it was *not* OK. He repeated that a dozen times, with a face that had gone beety, "For the love of Pete, Greg, get realistic. What's the use of adhering to the letter of the specifications and watching the test go to pot? It's about time you got the red tape out of your pants and went to work."

"I'm only saying," said Gregory Powell, patiently, as one explaining electronics to an idiot child, "that according to spec, those robots are equipped for asteroid mining without supervision. We're not supposed to watch them."

"All right. Look—logic!" He lifted his hairy fingers and pointed. "One: That new robot passed every test in the home laboratories. Two: United States Robots guaranteed their passing the test of actual performance on an asteroid. Three: The robots are not passing said tests. Four: If they don't pass, United States Robots loses ten million credits in cash and about one hundred million in reputation. Five: If they don't pass and we can't explain why they don't pass, it is just possible two good jobs may have to be bidden a fond farewell."

Powell groaned heavily behind a noticeably insincere smile. The unwritten motto of United States Robots and Mechanical Men Corporation was well-known: "No employee makes the same mistake twice. He is fired the first time."

Aloud he said, "You're as lucid as Euclid with everything except the facts. You've watched that robot group for three shifts, you redhead, and they did their work perfectly. You said so yourself. What else can we do?"

"Find out what's wrong, that's what we can do. So they did work perfectly when I watched them. But on three different occasions when I didn't watch them, they didn't bring in any ore. They didn't even come back on schedule. I had to go after them."

"And was anything wrong?"

"Not a thing. Not a thing. Everything was perfect. Smooth and perfect as the luminiferous ether. Only one little insignificant detail disturbed me—*there was no ore.*"

Powell scowled at the ceiling and pulled at his brown mustache. "I'll tell you what, Mike. We've been stuck with pretty lousy jobs in our time, but this takes the iridium asteroid. The whole business is complicated past endurance. Look, that robot, DV-5, has six robots under it. And not just under it—they're part of it."

"I know that—"

"Shut up!" said Powell, savagely, "I know you know it, but I'm just describing for the hell of it. Those six subsidiaries are part of DV-5 like your fingers are part of you and it gives them their orders neither by voice nor radio, but directly through positronic fields. Now—there isn't a roboticist back at United States Robots that knows what a positronic field is or how it works. And neither do I. Neither do you."

"The last," agreed Donovan, philosophically, "I know."

"Then look at our position. If everything works—fine! If anything goes wrong—we're out of our depth and there probably isn't a thing we can do, or anybody else. But the job belongs to us and not to anyone else so we're on the spot, Mike." He blazed away for a moment in silence. Then, "All right, have you got him outside?"

"Yes."

"Is everything normal now?"

"Well he hasn't got religious mania, and he isn't running around in a circle spouting Gilbert and Sullivan, so I suppose he's normal."

Donovan passed out the door, shaking his head viciously.

Powell reached for the "Handbook of Robotics" that weighed down one side of his desk to a near-founder and opened it reverently. He had once jumped out of the window of a burning house dressed only in shorts and the "Handbook." In a pinch, he would have skipped the shorts.

The "Handbook" was propped up before him, when Robot DV-5 entered, with Donovan kicking the door shut behind him.

Powell said somberly, "Hi, Dave. How do you feel?"

"Fine," said the robot. "Mind if I sit down?" He dragged up the specially reinforced chair that was his, and folded gently into it.

Powell regarded Dave—laymen might think of robots by their serial numbers; roboticists never—with approval. It was not overmassive by any means, in spite of its construction as thinking-unit of an integrated seven-unit robot team. It was seven feet tall, and a half-ton of metal and electricity. A lot? Not when that half-ton has to be a mass of condensers, circuits, relays, and vacuum cells that can handle practically any psychological reaction known to humans. And a positronic brain, which with ten pounds of matter and a few quintillions of positrons runs the whole show.

Powell groped in his shift pocket for a loose cigarette.

"Dave," he said, "you're a good fellow. There's nothing flighty or prima donnaish about you. You're a stable, rock-bottom mining robot, except that you're equipped to handle six subsidiaries in direct coordination. As far as I know, that has not introduced any unstable paths in your brain-path map."

The robot nodded; "That makes me feel swell, but what are you getting at, boss?" He was equipped with an excellent diaphragm, and the presence of overtones in the sound unit robbed him of much of that metallic flatness that marks the usual robot voice.

"I'm going to tell you. With all that in your favor, what's going wrong with your job? For instance, today's B-shift?"

Dave hesitated, "As far as I know, nothing."

"You didn't produce any ore."

"I know."

"Well, then——"

Dave was having trouble, "I can't explain that, boss. It's been giving me a case of nerves, or it would if I let it. My subsidiaries worked smoothly. I know I did." He considered, his photoelectric eyes glowing intensely. Then, "I don't remember. The day ended and there was Mike and there were the ore cars, mostly empty."

Donovan broke in, "You didn't report at shift-end those days, Dave. You know that?"

"I know. But as to why——" He shook his head slowly and ponderously.

Powell had the queasy feeling that if the robot's face were capable of expression, it would be one of pain and mortification. A robot, by its very nature, cannot bear to fail its function.

Donovan dragged his chair up to Powell's desk and leaned over, "Amnesia, do you think?"

"Can't say. But there's no use in trying to pin disease names on this. Human disorders apply to robots only as romantic analogies. They're no help to robotic engineering." He scratched his neck, "I hate to put him through the elementary brain-reaction tests. It won't help his self-respect any."

He looked at Dave thoughtfully and then at the Field-Test outline given in the "Handbook." He said, "See here, Dave, what about sitting through a test? It would be the wise thing to do."

The robot rose, "If you say so, boss." There *was* pain in his voice.

It started simply enough. Robot DV-5 multiplied five-place figures to the heartless ticking of a stop watch. He recited the prime numbers between a thousand and ten thousand. He extracted cube roots and integrated functions of varying complexity. He went through mechanical reactions in order of increasing difficulty. And, finally, worked his precise mechanical mind over the highest function of the robot world—the solutions of problems in judgment and ethics.

At the end of two hours, Powell was copiously besweated. Donovan had enjoyed a none-too-nutritious diet of fingernail and the robot said, "How does it look, boss?"

Powell said, "I've got to think it over, Dave. Snap judgments won't help much. Suppose you go back to the C-shift. Take it easy. Don't press too hard for quota just for a while—and we'll fix things up."

The robot left. Donovan looked at Powell.

"Well—"

Powell seemed determined to push up his mustache by the roots. He said, "There is nothing wrong with the currents of his positronic brain."

"I'd hate to be that certain."

"Oh, Jupiter, Mike! The brain is the surest part of a robot. It's quintuple-checked back on Earth. If they pass the field test perfectly, the way Dave did, there just isn't a chance of brain misfunction. That test covered every key path in the brain."

"So where are we?"

"Don't rush me. Let me work this out. There's still the possibility of a mechanical breakdown in the body. That leaves about fifteen hundred condensers, twenty thousand individual electric circuits, five hundred vacuum cells, a thousand relays, and upty-ump thousand other individual pieces of complexity that can be wrong. *And* these mysterious positronic fields no one knows anything about."

"Listen, Greg," Donovan grew desperately urgent. "I've got an idea. That robot may be lying. He never—"

"Robots can't knowingly lie, you fool. Now if we had the McCormack-Wesley tester, we could check each individual item in his body within twenty-four to forty-eight hours, but the only two M.-W. testers existing are on Earth, and they weigh ten tons, are on concrete foundations and can't be moved. Isn't that peachy?"

Donovan pounded the desk, "But, Greg, he only goes wrong when we're not around. There's something—sinister—about—that." He punctuated the sentence with slams of fist against desk.

"You," said Powell, slowly, "make me sick. You've been reading adventure novels."

"What I want to know," shouted Donovan, "is what we're going to do about it."

"I'll tell you. I'm going to install a visiplate right over my desk. Right on the wall over there, see!" He jabbed a vicious finger at the spot. "Then I'm going to focus it at whatever part of the mine is being worked, and I'm going to watch. That's all."

"That's all? Greg—"

Powell rose from his chair and leaned his balled fists on the desk, "Mike, I'm having a hard time." His voice was weary. "For a week, you've been plaguing me about Dave. You say he's gone wrong. Do you know how he's gone wrong? No! Do you know what shape this wrongness takes? No! Do you know what brings it on? No! Do you know what snaps him out? No! Do you know anything about it?

No! Do I know anything about it? No! So what do you want me to do?"

Donovan's arm swept outward in a vague, grandiose gesture, "You got me!"

"So I tell you again. Before we do anything toward a cure, we've got to find out what the disease is in the first place. The first step in cooking rabbit stew is catching the rabbit. Well, we've got to catch that rabbit! Now get out of here."

Donovan stared at the preliminary outline of his field report with weary eyes. For one thing, he was tired and for another, what was there to report while things were unsettled? He felt resentful.

He said, "Greg, we're almost a thousand tons behind schedule."

"You," replied Powell, never looking up, "are telling me something I don't know."

"What I want to know," said Donovan, in sudden savagery, "is why we're always tangled up with new-type robots. I've finally decided that the robots that were good enough for my great-uncle on my mother's side are good enough for me. I'm for what's tried and true. The test of time is what counts—good, solid, old-fashioned robots that never go wrong."

Powell threw a book with perfect aim, and Donovan went tumbling off his seat.

"Your job," said Powell, evenly, "for the last five years has been to test new robots under actual working conditions for United States Robots. Because you and I have been so injudicious as to display proficiency at the task, we've been rewarded with the dirtiest jobs. That," he jabbed holes in the air with his finger in Donovan's direction, "is your work. You've been griping about it, from personal memory, since about five minutes after United States Robots signed you up. Why don't you resign?"

"Well, I'll tell you." Donovan rolled onto his stomach,

and took a firm grip on his wild, red hair to hold his head up. "There's a certain principle involved. After all, as a trouble shooter, I've played a part in the development of new robots. There's the principle of aiding scientific advance. But don't get me wrong. It's not the principle that keeps me going; it's the money they pay us. *Greg!*"

Powell jumped at Donovan's wild shout, and his eyes followed the redhead's to the visiplate, when they goggled in fixed horror. He whispered, "Holy—howling—Jupiter!"

Donovan scrambled breathlessly to his feet, "Look at them, Greg. They've gone nuts."

Powell said, "Get a pair of suits. We're going out there."

He watched the posturings of the robots on the visiplate. They were bronzy gleams of smooth motion against the shadowy crags of the airless asteroid. There was a marching formation now, and in their own dim body light, the rough-hewn walls of the mine tunnel swam past noiselessly, checkered with misty erratic blobs of shadow. They marched in unison, seven of them, with Dave at the head. They wheeled and turned in macabre simultaneity; and melted through changes of formation with the weird ease of chorus dancers in Lunar Bowl.

Donovan was back with the suits. "They've gone jingo on us, Greg. That's a military march."

"For all you know," was the cold response, "it may be a series of calisthenic exercises. Or Dave may be under the hallucination of being a dancing master. Just you think first, and don't bother to speak afterward, either."

Donovan scowled and slipped a detonator into the empty side holster with an ostentatious shove. He said, "Anyway, there you are. So we work with new-model robots. It's our job, granted. But answer me one question. Why . . . *why* does something invariably go wrong with them?"

"Because," said Powell, somberly, "we are accursed. Let's go!"

• • •

Far ahead through the thick velvety blackness of the corridors that reached past the illuminated circles of their flashlights, robot light twinkled.

"There they are," breathed Donovan.

Powell whispered tensely, "I've been trying to get him by radio but he doesn't answer. The radio circuit is probably out."

"Then I'm glad the designers haven't worked out robots who can work in total darkness yet. I'd hate to have to find seven mad robots in a black pit without radio communication, if they *weren't* lit up like blasted radioactive Christmas trees."

"Crawl up on the ledge above, Mike. They're coming this way, and I want to watch them at close range. Can you make it?"

Donovan made the jump with a grunt. Gravity was considerably below Earth-normal, but with a heavy suit, the advantage was not too great, and the ledge meant a near ten-foot jump. Powell followed.

The column of robots were trailing Dave single-file. In mechanical rhythm, they converted to double and returned to single in different order. It was repeated over and over again and Dave never turned his head.

Dave was within twenty feet when the play-acting ceased. The subsidiary robots broke formation, waited a moment, then clattered off into the distance—very rapidly. Dave looked after them, then slowly sat down. He rested his head in one hand in a very human gesture.

His voice sounded in Powell's earphones, "Are you here, boss?"

Powell beckoned to Donovan and hopped off the ledge.

"O.K., Dave, what's been going on?"

The robot shook his head, "I don't know. One moment I was handling a tough outcropping in Tunnel 17, and the next I was aware of humans close by, and I found myself half a mile down main-stem."

"Where are the subsidiaries now?" asked Donovan.

"Back at work, of course. How much time has been lost?"

"Not much. Forget it." Then to Donovan, Powell added, "Stay with him the rest of the shift. Then, come back. I've a couple of ideas."

It was three hours before Donovan returned. He looked tired.

Powell said, "How did it go?"

Donovan shrugged wearily, "Nothing ever goes wrong when you watch them. Throw me a butt, will you?"

The redhead lit it with exaggerated care and blew a careful smoke ring. He said, "I've been working it out, Greg. You know, Dave had a queer background for a robot. There are six others under him in an extreme regimentation. He's got life and death power over those subsidiary robots and it must react on his mentality. Suppose he finds it necessary to emphasize this power as a concession to his ego."

"Get to the point."

"It's right here. Suppose we have militarism. Suppose he's fashioning himself an army. Suppose he's training them in military maneuvers. Suppose—"

"Suppose you go soak your head. Your nightmares must be in technicolor. You're postulating a major aberration of the positronic brain. If your analysis were correct, Dave would have to break down the First Law of Robotics: that a robot may not injure a human being or, through inaction allow a human being to be injured. The type of militaristic attitude and domineering ego you propose must have as the end-point of its logical implications, domination of humans."

"All right. How do you know that isn't the fact of the matter?"

"Because any robot with a brain like that would, one,

never have left the factory, and two, be spotted immediately if it ever was. I tested Dave, you know."

Powell shoved his chair back and put his feet on the desk. "No. We're still in the position where we can't make our stew because we haven't the slightest notion as to what's wrong. For instance, if we could find out what that *danse macabre* we witnessed was all about, we would be on the way out."

He paused, "Now listen, Mike, how does this sound to you? Dave goes wrong only when neither of us is present. And when he is wrong, the arrival of either of us snaps him out of it."

"I once told you that was sinister."

"Don't interrupt. How is a robot different when humans are not present? The answer is obvious. There is a larger requirement of persona initiative. In that case, look for the body parts that are affected by the new requirements."

"Golly." Donovan sat up straight, then subsided. "No, no. Not enough. It's too broad. It doesn't cut the possibilities much."

"Can't help that. In any case, there's no danger of not making quota. We'll take shifts watching those robots through the visor. Any time anything goes wrong, we get to the scene of action immediately. That will put them right."

"But the robots will fail spec anyway, Greg. United States Robots can't market DV models with a report like that."

"Obviously. We've got to locate the error in make-up and correct it—and we've got ten days to do it in." Powell scratched his head. "The trouble is . . . well, you had better look at the blueprints yourself."

The blueprints covered the floor like a carpet and Donovan crawled over the face of them following Powell's erratic pencil.

Powell said, "Here's where you come in, Mike. You're the body specialist, and I want you to check me. I've been trying to cut out all circuits not involved in the personal initiative hookup. Right here, for instance, is the trunk artery involving mechanical operations. I cut out all routine side routes as emergency divisions—" He looked up, "What do you think?"

Donovan had a very bad taste in his mouth, "The job's not that simple, Greg. Personal initiative isn't an electric circuit you can separate from the rest and study. When a robot is on his own, the intensity of the body activity increases immediately on almost all fronts. There isn't a circuit entirely unaffected. What must be done is to locate the particular condition—a very specific condition—that throws him off, and *then* start eliminating circuits."

Powell got up and dusted himself, "Hmph. All right. Take away the blueprints and burn them."

Donovan said, "You see when activity intensifies, anything can happen, given one single faulty part. Insulation breaks down, a condenser spills over, a connection sparks, a coil overheats. And if you work blind, with the whole robot to choose from, you'll never find the bad spot. If you take Dave apart and test every point of his body mechanism one by one, putting him together each time, and trying him out—"

"All right. All right. I can see through a porthole, too."

They faced each other hopelessly, and then Powell said cautiously, "Suppose we interview one of the subsidiaries."

Neither Powell nor Donovan had ever had previous occasion to talk to a "finger." It could talk; it wasn't quite the perfect analogy to a human finger. In fact, it had a fairly developed brain, but that brain was tuned primarily to the reception of orders via positronic field, and its reaction to independent stimuli was rather fumbling.

Nor was Powell certain as to its name. Its serial number was DV-5-2, but that was not very useful.

He compromised. "Look, pal," he said, "I'm going to ask you to do some hard thinking and then you can go back to your boss."

The "finger" nodded its head stiffly, but did not exert its limited brain-power on speech.

"Now on four occasions recently," Powell said, "your boss deviated from brainscheme. Do you remember those occasions?"

"Yes, sir."

Donovan growled angrily, "*He* remembers. I tell you there is something very sinister—"

"Oh, go bash your skull. Of course, the 'finger' remembers. There is nothing wrong with him." Powell turned back to the robot, "What were you doing each time . . . I mean the whole group."

The "finger" had a curious air of reciting by rote, as if he answered questions by the mechanical pressure of his brain pan, but without any enthusiasm whatever.

He said, "The first time we were at work on a difficult outcropping in Tunnel 17, Level B. The second time we were buttressing the roof against a possible cave-in. The third time we were preparing accurate blasts in order to tunnel farther without breaking into a subterranean fissure. The fourth time was just after a minor cave in."

"What happened at these times?"

"It is difficult to describe. An order would be issued, but before we could receive and interpret it, a new order came to march in queer formation."

Powell snapped out, "Why?"

"I don't know."

Donovan broke in tensely, "What was the first order . . . the one that was superseded by the marching directions?"

"I don't know. I sensed that an order was sent, but there was never time to receive it."

"Could you tell us anything about it? Was it the same order each time?"

The "finger" shook his head unhappily, "I don't know."

Powell leaned back, "All right, get back to your boss."

The "finger" left, with visible relief.

Donovan said, "Well, we accomplished a lot that time. That was real sharp dialogue all the way through. Listen, Dave and that imbecile 'finger' are both holding out on us. There is too much they don't know and don't remember. We've got to stop trusting them, Greg."

Powell brushed his mustache the wrong way, "So help me, Mike, another fool remark out of you, and I'll take away your rattle and teething ring."

"All right. You're the genius of the team. I'm just a poor sucker. Where do we stand?"

"Right behind the eight ball. I tried to work it backward through the 'finger,' and couldn't. So we've got to work it forward."

"A great man," marveled Donovan. "How simple that makes it. Now translate that into English, Master."

"Translating it into baby talk would suit you better. I mean that we've got to find out what order it is that Dave gives just before everything goes black. It would be the key to the business."

"And how do you expect to do that? We can't get close to him because nothing will go wrong as long as we are there. We can't catch the orders by radio because they are transmitted via this positronic field. That eliminates the close-range and the long-range method, leaving us a neat, cozy zero."

"By direct observation, yes. There's still deduction."

"Huh?"

"We're going on shifts, Mike." Powell smiled grimly. "And we are not taking our eyes off the visiplate. We're going to watch every action of those steel headaches. When they go off into their act, we're going to see what happened immediately before and we're going to deduce the order."

Donovan opened his mouth and left it that way for a full minute. Then he said in strangled tones, "I resign. I quit."

"You have ten days to think up something better," said Powell wearily.

Which, for eight days, Donovan tried mightily to do. For

eight days, on alternate four-hour shifts, he watched with aching and bleary eyes those glinty metallic forms move against the vague background. And for eight days in the four-hour in-betweens, he cursed United States Robots, the DV models, and the day he was born.

And then on the eighth day, when Powell entered with an aching head and sleepy eyes for his shift, Donovan stood up and with very careful and deliberate aim launched a heavy book end for the exact center of the visiplate. There was a very appropriate splintering noise.

Powell gasped, "What did you do that for?"

"Because," said Donovan, almost calmly, "I'm not watching it any more. We've got two days left and we haven't found out a thing. DV-5 is a lousy loss. He's stopped five times since I've been watching and three times on your shift, and I can't make out what orders he gave, and you couldn't make it out. And I don't believe you could ever make it out because I know I couldn't ever."

"Jumping Space, how can you watch six robots at the same time? One makes with the hands, and one with the feet, and one like a windmill and another is jumping up and down like a maniac. And the other two . . . devil knows what they are doing. And then they all stop. So! So!"

"Greg, we're not doing it right. We got to get up close. We've got to watch what they're doing from where we can see the details."

Powell broke a bitter silence. "Yeah, and wait for something to go wrong with only two days to go."

"Is it any better watching from here?"

"It's more comfortable."

"Ah— But there's something you can do there that you can't do here."

"What's that?"

"You can make them stop—at whatever time you choose—and while you're prepared and watching to see what goes wrong."

Powell startled into alertness, "Howzzat?"

"Well, figure it out yourself. You're the brains you say. Ask yourself some questions. When does DV-5 go out of whack? When did that 'finger' say he did? When a cave-in threatened, or actually occurred, when delicately measured explosives were being laid down, when a difficult seam was hit."

"In other words, during emergencies." Powell was excited.

"Right! When *did* you expect it to happen! It's the personal initiative factor that's giving us the trouble. And it's just during emergencies in the absence of a human being that personal initiative is most strained. Now what is the logical deduction? How can we create our own stoppage when and where we want it?" He paused triumphantly—he was beginning to enjoy his role—and answered his own question to forestall the obvious answer on Powell's tongue. "By creating our own emergency."

Powell said, "Mike—you're right."

"Thanks, pal. I knew I'd do it some day."

"All right, and skip the sarcasm. We'll save it for Earth, and preserve it in jars for future long, cold winters. Meanwhile, what emergency can we create?"

"We could flood the mines, if this weren't an airless asteroid."

"A witticism, no doubt," said Powell. "Really, Mike, you'll incapacitate me with laughter. What about a mild cave-in?"

Donovan pursed his lips and said, "O.K. by me."

"Good. Let's get started."

Powell felt uncommonly like a conspirator as he wound his way over the craggy landscape. His sub-gravity walk teetered across the broken ground, kicking rocks to right and left under his weight in noiseless puffs of gray dust. Mentally, though, it was the cautious crawl of the plotter.

He said, "Do you know where they are?"

"I think so, Greg."

"All right," Powell said gloomily, "but if any 'finger'

gets within twenty feet of us, we'll be sensed whether we are in the line of sight or not. I hope you know that."

"When I need an elementary course in robotics, I'll file an application with you, formally, and in triplicate. Down through here."

They were in the tunnels now; even the starlight was gone. The two hugged the walls, flashes flickering out the way in intermittent bursts. Powell felt for the security of his detonator.

"Do you know this tunnel, Mike?"

"Not so good. It's a new one. I think I can make it out from what I saw in the visiplate, though—"

Interminable minutes passed, and then Mike said, "Feel that!"

There was a slight vibration thrumming the wall against the fingers of Powell's metal-incased hand. There was no sound, naturally.

"Blasting! We're pretty close."

"Keep your eyes open," said Powell.

Donovan nodded impatiently.

It was upon them and gone before they could seize themselves—just a bronze glint across the field of vision. They clung together in silence.

Powell whispered, "Think it sensed us?"

"Hope not. But we'd better flank them. Take the first side tunnel to the right."

"Suppose we miss them altogether?"

"Well what do you want to do? Go back?" Donovan grunted fiercely. "They're within a quarter of a mile. I was watching them through the visiplate, wasn't I? And we've got two days—"

"Oh, shut up. You're wasting your oxygen. Is this a side passage here?" The flash flicked. "It is. Let's go."

The vibration was considerably more marked and the ground below shuddered uneasily.

"This is good," said Donovan, "if it doesn't give out on us, though." He flung his light ahead anxiously.

They could touch the roof of the tunnel with a half-up-stretched hand, and the bracings had been newly replaced.

Donovan hesitated, "Dead end, let's go back."

"No. Hold on." Powell squeezed clumsily past. "Is that light ahead?"

"Light? I don't see any. Where would there be light down here?"

"Robot light." He was scrambling up a gentle incline on hands and knees. His voice was hoarse and anxious in Donovan's ears. "Hey, Mike, come up here."

There was light. Donovan crawled up and over Powell's outstretched legs. "An opening?"

"Yes. They must be working into this tunnel from the other side now—I think."

Donovan felt the ragged edges of the opening that looked out into what the cautious flashlight showed to be a larger and obviously main-stem tunnel. The hole was too small for a man to go through, almost too small for two men to look through simultaneously.

"There's nothing there," said Donovan.

"Well, not now. But there must have been a second ago or we wouldn't have seen light. Watch out!"

The walls rolled about them and they felt the impact. A fine dust showered down. Powell lifted a cautious head and looked again. "All right, Mike. They're there."

The glittering robots clustered fifty feet down the main stem. Metal arms labored mightily at the rubbish heap brought down by the last blast.

Donovan urged eagerly, "Don't waste time. It won't be long before they get through, and the next blast may get us."

"For Pete's sake, don't rush me." Powell unlimbered the detonator, and his eyes searched anxiously across the dusky background where the only light was robot light and it was impossible to tell a projecting boulder from a shadow.

"There's a spot in the roof, see it, almost over them. The

last blast didn't quite get it. If you can get it at the base, half the roof will cave in."

Powell followed the dim finger, "Check! Now fasten your eye on the robots and pray they don't move too far from that part of the tunnel. They're my light sources. Are all seven there?"

Donovan counted, "All seven."

"Well, then, watch them. Watch every motion!"

His detonator was lifted and remained poised while Donovan watched and cursed and blinked the sweat out of his eye.

It flashed!

There was a jar, a series of hard vibrations, and then a jarring thump that threw Powell heavily against Donovan.

Donovan yowled, "Greg, you threw me off. I didn't see a thing."

Powell stared about wildly, "Where are they?"

Donovan fell into a stupid silence. There was no sign of the robots. It was dark as the depths of the River Styx.

"Think we buried them?" quavered Donovan.

"Let's get down there. Don't ask me what I think." Powell crawled backward at tumbling speed.

"Mike!"

Donovan paused in the act of following. "What's wrong now?"

"Hold on!" Powell's breathing was rough and irregular in Donovan's ears. "Mike! Do you hear me, Mike?"

"I'm right here. What is it?"

"We're blocked in. It wasn't the ceiling coming down fifty feet away that knocked us over. It was our own ceiling. The shock's tumbled it!"

"What!" Donovan scrambled up against a hard barrier. "Turn on the flash."

Powell did so. At no point was there room for a rabbit to squeeze through. Donovan said softly, "Well, what do you know?"

• • •

They wasted a few moments and some muscular power in an effort to move the blocking barrier. Powell varied this by wrenching at the edges of the original hole. For a moment, Powell lifted his blaster. But in those close quarters, a flash would be suicide and he knew it. He sat down.

"You know, Mike," he said, "we've really messed this up. We are no nearer finding out what's wrong with Dave. It was a good idea but it blew up in our face."

Donovan's glance was bitter with an intensity totally wasted on the darkness. "I hate to disturb you, old man, but quite apart from what we know or don't know of Dave, we're slightly trapped. If we don't get loose, fella, we're going to die. D-I-E, die. How much oxygen have we anyway? Not more than six hours."

"I've thought of that." Powell's fingers went up to his long-suffering mustache and clanged uselessly against the transparent visor. "Of course, we could get Dave to dig us out easily in that time, except that our precious emergency must have thrown him off, and his radio circuit is out."

"And isn't that nice?"

Donovan edged up to the opening and managed to get his metal-incased head out. It was an extremely tight fit.

"Hey, Greg!"

"What?"

"Suppose we get Dave within twenty feet. He'll snap to normal. That will save us."

"Sure, but where is he?"

"Down the corridor—way down. For Pete's sake, stop pulling before you drag my head out of its socket. I'll give you your chance to look."

Powell maneuvered his head outside, "We did it all right. Look at those saps. That must be a ballet they're doing."

"Never mind the side remarks. Are they getting any closer?"

"Can't tell yet. They're too far away. Give me a chance.

Pass me my flash, will you? I'll try to attract their attention that way."

He gave up after two minutes, "Not a chance! They must be blind. Uh-oh, they're starting toward us. What do you know?"

Donovan said, "Hey, let me see!"

There was a silent scuffle. Powell said, "All right!" and Donovan got his head out.

They were approaching. Dave was high-stepping the way in front and the six "fingers" were a weaving chorus line behind him.

Donovan marveled, "What are they doing? That's what I want to know. It looks like the Virginia reel—and Dave's a major-domo, or I never saw one."

"Oh, leave me alone with your descriptions," grumbled Powell. "How near are they?"

"Within fifty feet and coming this way. We'll be out in fifteen min— Uh—huh—HUH—HEY-Y!"

"What's going on?" It took Powell several seconds to recover from his stunned astonishment at Donovan's vocal gyrations. "Come on, give me a chance at that hole. Don't be a hog about it."

He fought his way upward, but Donovan kicked wildly. "They did an about-face, Greg. They're leaving. Dave! Hey, Da-a-ave!"

Powell shrieked, "What's the use of that, you fool? Sound won't carry."

"Well, then," panted Donovan, "kick the walls, slam them, get some vibration started. We've got to attract their attention somehow, Greg, or we're through." He pounded like a madman.

Powell shook him, "Wait, Mike, wait. Listen, I've got an idea. Jumping Jupiter, this is a fine time to get around to the simple solutions. Mike!"

"What do you want?" Donovan pulled his head in.

"Let me in there fast before they get out of range."

"Out of range! What are you going to do? Hey, what are

you going to do with that detonator?" He grabbed Powell's arm.

Powell shook off the grip violently. "I'm going to do a little shooting."

"Why?"

"That's for later. Let's see if it works first. If it doesn't, then— Get out of the way and let me shoot!"

The robots were flickers, small and getting smaller, in the distance. Powell lined up the sights tensely, and pulled the trigger three times. He lowered the guns and peered anxiously. One of the subsidiaries was down! There were only six gleaming figures now.

Powell called into his transmitter uncertainly, "Dave!"

A pause, then the answer sounded to both men, "Boss? Where are you? My third subsidiary has had his chest blown in. He's out of commission."

"Never mind your subsidiary," said Powell. "We're trapped in a cave-in where you were blasting. Can you see our flashlight?"

"Sure. We'll be right there."

Powell sat back and relaxed. "That, my fran', is that."

Donovan said very softly with tears in his voice, "All right, Greg. You win. I beat my forehead against the ground before your feet. Now don't feed me any bull. Just tell me quietly what it's all about."

"Easy. It's just that all through we missed the obvious— as usual. We knew it was the personal initiative circuit, and that it always happened during emergencies, but we kept looking for a specific order as the cause. Why should it be an order?"

"Why not?"

"Well, look. Why not a type of order. What type of order requires the most initiative? What type of order would occur almost always only in an emergency?"

"Don't ask me, Greg. Tell me!"

"I'm doing it! It's the six-way order. Under all ordinary

conditions, one or more of the 'fingers' would be doing routine tasks requiring no close supervision—in the sort of offhand way our bodies handle the routine walking motions. But in an emergency, all six subsidiaries must be mobilized immediately and simultaneously. Dave must handle six robots at a time and something gives. The rest was easy. Any decrease in initiative required, such as the arrival of humans, snaps him back. So I destroyed one of the robots. When I did, he was transmitting only five-way orders. Initiative decreases—he's normal."

"How did you get all that?" demanded Donovan.

"Just logical guessing. I tried it and it worked."

The robot's voice was in their ears again, "Here I am. Can you hold out half an hour?"

"Easy!" said Powell. Then, to Donovan, he continued, "And now the job should be simple. We'll go through the circuits, and check off each part that gets an extra workout in a six-way order as against a five-way. How big a field does that leave us?"

Donovan considered, "Not much, I think. If Dave is like the preliminary model we saw back at the factory, there's no special co-ordinating circuit that would be the only section involved." He cheered up suddenly and amazingly, "Say, that wouldn't be bad at all. There's nothing to that."

"All right. You think it over and we'll check the blueprints when we get back. And now, till Dave reaches us, I'm relaxing."

"Hey, wait! Just tell me one thing. What were those queer shifting marches, those funny dance steps, that the robots went through every time they went screwy?"

"That? I don't know. But I've got a notion. Remember, those subsidiaries were Dave's 'fingers.' We were always saying that, you know. Well, it's my idea that in all these interludes, whenever Dave became a psychiatric case, he went off into a moronic maze, spending his time *twiddling his fingers*."

BLIND ALLEY

Only once in Galactic History was an intelligent race of non-Humans discovered—
"Essays on History,"
by Ligurn Vier

I.

From: Bureau for the Outer Provinces
To: Loodun Antyok, Chief Public Administrator, A-8

Subject: Civilian Supervisor of Cepheus 18, Administrative Position as,
References:

(a) Act of Council 2515, of the year 971 of the Galactic Empire, entitled, "Appointment of Official of the Administrative Service, Methods for, Revision of."

(b) Imperial Directive, Ja 2374, dated 243/975 G.E.

1. By authorization of reference (a), you are hereby appointed to the subject position. The authority of said position as Civilian Supervisor of Cepheus 18 will extend over non-Human subjects of the Emperor living upon the planet under the terms of autonomy set forth in reference (b).

2. The duties of the subject position shall comprise the general supervision of all non-Human internal affairs, co-ordination of authorized government investigating and reporting committees, and the preparation

of semiannual reports on all phases of non-Human affairs.

C. Morily, Chief, BuOuProv,
12/977 G.E.

Loodun Antyok had listened carefully, and now he shook his round head mildly, "Friend, I'd like to help you, but you've grabbed the wrong dog by the ears. You'd better take this up with the Bureau."

Tomor Zammo flung himself back into his chair, rubbed his beak of a nose fiercely, thought better of whatever he was going to say, and answered quietly, "Logical, but not practical. I can't make a trip to Trantor now. You're the Bureau's representative on Cepheus 18. Are you entirely helpless?"

"Well, even as Civilian Supervisor, I've got to work within the limits of Bureau policy."

"Good," Zammo cried, "then, tell me what Bureau policy is. I head a scientific investigating committee, under direct Imperial authorization with, supposedly, the widest powers; yet at every angle in the road I am pulled up short by the civilian authorities with only the parrot shriek of 'Bureau policy' to justify themselves. What *is* Bureau policy? I haven't received a decent definition yet."

Antyok's gaze was level and unruffled. He said, "As I see it—and this is not official, so you can't hold me to it—Bureau policy consists in treating the non-Humans as decently as possible."

"Then, what authority have they—"

"*Ssh!* No use raising your voice. As a matter of fact, His Imperial Majesty is a humanitarian and a disciple of the philosophy of Aurelion. I can tell you quietly that it is pretty well-known that it is the Emperor himself who first suggested that this world be established. You can bet that Bureau policy will stick pretty close to Imperial notions. And you can bet that I can't paddle my way against *that* sort of current."

"Well, m'boy," the physiologist's fleshy eyelids quivered, "if you take that sort of attitude, you're going to lose your job. No, I won't have you kicked out. That's not what I mean at all. Your job will just fade out from under you; because nothing is going to be accomplished here!"

"Really? Why?" Antyok was short, pink, and pudgy, and his plump-cheeked face usually found it difficult to put on display any expression other than one of bland and cheerful politeness—but it looked grave now.

"You haven't been here long. I have." Zammo scowled. "Mind if I smoke?" The cigar in his hand was gnarled and strong and was puffed to life carelessly.

He continued roughly, "There's no place here for humanitarianism, administrator. You're treating non-Humans as if they were Humans, and it won't work. In fact, I don't like the word 'non-Human.' They're animals."

"They're intelligent," interjected Antyok, softly.

"Well, intelligent animals, then. I presume the two terms are not mutually exclusive. Alien intelligences mingling in the same space won't work, anyway."

"Do you propose killing them off?"

"Galaxy, no!" He gestured with his cigar. "I propose we look upon them as objects for study, and only that. We could learn a good deal from these animals if we were allowed to. Knowledge, I might point out, that would be used for the immediate benefit of the human race. *There's* humanity for you. *There's* the good of the masses, if it's this spineless cult of Aurelion that interests you."

"What, for instance, do you refer to?"

"To take the most obvious—You have heard of their chemistry, I take it?"

"Yes," Antyok admitted. "I have leafed through most of the reports on the non-Humans published in the last ten years. I expect to go through more."

"Hmp. Well— Then, all I need say is that their chemical therapy is extremely thorough. For instance, I have witnessed personally the healing of a broken bone—what passes for a broken bone with them, I mean—by the use of a pill. The bone was whole in fifteen minutes. Naturally, none of their drugs are any earthly use on Humans. Most would kill quickly. But if we found out how they worked on the non-Humans—on the animals—"

"Yes, yes. I see the significance."

"Oh, you do. Come, that's gratifying. A second point is that these animals communicate in an unknown manner."

"Telepathy!"

The scientist's mouth twisted, as he ground out, "Telepathy! Telepathy! Telepathy! Might as well say by witch brew. Nobody knows anything about telepathy except its name. What is the mechanism of telepathy? What is the physiology and the physics of it? I would like to find out, but I can't. Bureau policy, if I listen to you, forbids."

Antyok's little mouth pursed itself. "But— Pardon me, doctor, but I don't follow you. How are you prevented? Surely the Civil Administration has made no attempt to hamper scientific investigation of these non-Humans. I cannot speak for my predecessor entirely, of course, but I myself—"

"No direct interference has occurred. I don't speak of that. But by the Galaxy, administrator, we're hampered by the spirit of the entire set-up. You're making us deal with humans. You allow them their own leader and internal autonomy. You pamper them and give them what Aurelion's philosophy would call 'rights.' I can't deal with their leader."

"Why not?"

"Because he refuses to allow me a free hand. He refuses to allow experiments on any subject without the subject's own consent. The two or three volunteers we get are not too bright. It's an impossible arrangement."

Antyok shrugged helplessly.

Zammo continued, "In addition, it is obviously impossible to learn anything of value concerning the brains, physiology, and chemistry of these animals without dissection, dietary experiments, and drugs. You know, administrator, scientific investigation is a hard game. Humanity hasn't much place in it."

Loodun Antyok tapped his chin with a doubtful finger, "Must it be quite so hard? These are harmless creatures, these non-Humans. Surely, dissection— Perhaps, if you were to approach them a bit differently—I have the idea that you antagonize them. Your attitude might be somewhat overbearing."

"Overbearing! I am not one of these whining social psychologists who are all the fad these days. I don't believe you can solve a problem that requires dissection by approaching it with what is called the 'correct personal attitude' in the cant of the times."

"I'm sorry you think so. Sociopsychological training is required of all administrators above the grade of A-4."

Zammo withdrew his cud of a cigar from his mouth and replaced it after a suitably contemptuous interval. "Then you'd better use a bit of your technique on the Bureau. You know, I *do* have friends at the Imperial court."

"Well, now, I *can't* take the matter up with them, not baldly. Basic policy does not fall within my cognizance, and such things can only be initiated by the Bureau. But, you know, we might try an indirect approach on this." He smiled faintly, "Strategy."

"What sort?"

Antyok pointed a sudden finger, while his other hand fell lightly on the rows of gray-bound reports upon the floor just next to his chair. "Now, look, I've gone through most of these. They're dull, but contain *some* facts. For instance, when was the last non-Human infant born on Cepheus 18?"

Zammo spent little time in consideration. "Don't know. Don't care either."

"But the Bureau would. There's *never* been a non-Human infant born on Cepheus 18—not in the two years the world has been established. Do you know the reason?"

The physiologist shrugged, "Too many possible factors. It would take study."

"All right, then. Suppose you write a report—"

"Reports! I've written twenty."

"Write another. Stress the unsolved problems. Tell them you must change your methods. Harp on the birth-rate problem. The Bureau doesn't dare ignore that. If the non-Humans die out, someone will have to answer to the Emperor. You see—"

Zammo stared, his eyes dark. "That will swing it?"

"I've been working for the Bureau for twenty-seven years. I know its ways."

"I'll think about it." Zammo rose and stalked out of the office. The door slammed behind him.

It was later that Zammo said to a co-worker, "He's a bureaucrat, in the first place. He won't abandon the ortho- doxies of paper work and he won't risk sticking his neck out. He'll accomplish little by himself, yet maybe more than a little if we work through him."

From: Administrative Headquarters, Cepheus 18
To: BuOuProv
Subject: Outer Province Project 2563, Part II— Scientific Investigations of non-Human of Cepheus 18, Co-ordination of,
References:
(a) BuOuProv letr. Cep-N-Cm/jg, 100132, dated 302/975 G.E.
(b) AdHQ-Ceph 18 letr. AA-LA/mn, dated 140/ 977 G.E.
Enclosure:
1. SciGroup 10, Physical & Biochemical Divi- sion, Report, entitled, "Physiologic Characteristics of non-Humans of Cepheus 18, Part XI," dated 172/977 G.E.
1. Enclosure 1, included herewith, is forwarded for the information of the BuOuProv. It is to be noted that Section XII, paragraphs 1–16 of Encl. 1, concern possible changes in present BuOuProv policy with

regard to non-Humans with a view of facilitating physical and chemical investigations at present proceeding under authorization of reference (a).

2. It is brought to the attention of the BuOuProv that reference (b) has already discussed possible changes in investigating methods and that it remains the opinion of AdHQ-Ceph 18 that such changes are as yet premature. It is nevertheless suggested that the question of non-Human birth rate be made the subject of a BuOuProv project assigned to AdHQ-Ceph 18 in view of the importance attached by SciGroup 10 to the problem, as evidence in Section V of Enclosure 1.

L. Antyok, Superv, AdHQ-Ceph 18,
174/977

From: BuOuProv
To: AdHQ-Ceph 18
Subject: Outer Province Project 2563—Scientific Investigations of non-Humans of Cepheus 18, Coordination of,
References:

(a) AdHQ-Ceph 18 letr. AA-LA/mn, dated 174/977 G.E.

1. In response to the suggestion contained in paragraph 2 of reference (a), it is considered that the question of the non-Human birth rate does not fall within the cognizance of AdHQ-Ceph18. In view of the fact that SciGroup 10 has reported said sterility to be probably due to a chemical deficiency in the food supply, all investigations in the field are relegated to SciGroup 10 as the proper authority.

2. Investigating procedures by the various SciGroups shall continue according to current directives on the subject. No changes in policy are envisaged.

C. Morily, Chief, BuOuProv,
186/977 G.E.

II.

There was a loose-jointed gauntness about the news reporter which made him appear somberly tall. He was Gustiv Bannerd, with whose reputation was combined ability—two things which do not invariably go together despite the maxims of elementary morality.

Loodum Antyok took his measure doubtfully and said, "There's no use denying that you're right. But the SciGroup report was confidential. I don't understand how—"

"It leaked," said Bannerd, callously. "Everything leaks."

Antyok was obviously baffled, and his pink face furrowed slightly, "Then I'll just have to plug the leak here. I can't pass your story. All references to SciGroup complaints have to come out. You see that, don't you?"

"No." Bannerd was calm enough. "It's important; and I have my rights under the Imperial directive. I think the Empire should know what's going on."

"But it isn't going on," said Antyok, despairingly. "Your claims are all wrong. The Bureau isn't going to change its policy. I showed you the letters."

"You think you can stand up against Zammo when he puts the pressure on?" the newsman asked derisively.

"I will—if I think he's wrong."

"If!" stated Bannerd flatly. Then, in a sudden fervor, "Antyok, the Empire has something great here; something greater by a good deal than the government apparently realizes. They're destroying it. They're treating these creatures like animals."

"Really—" began Antyok, weakly.

"Don't talk about Cepheus 18. It's a zoo. It's a high-class zoo, with your petrified scientists teasing those poor creatures with their sticks poking through the bars. You throw them chunks of meat, but you cage them up. I know! I've been writing about them for two years now. I've almost been living with them."

"Zammo says—"

"Zammo!" This with hard contempt.

"Zammo says," insisted Antyok with worried firmness, "that we treat them too like humans as it is."

The newsman's straight, long cheeks were rigid, "Zammo is rather animallike in his own right. He is a science-worshipper. We can do with less of them. Have you read Aurelion's works?" The last was suddenly posed.

"Umm. Yes. I understand the Emperor—"

"The Emperor tends towards us. That is good—better than the hounding of the last reign."

"I don't see where you're heading?"

"These aliens have much to teach us. You understand? It is nothing that Zammo and his SciGroup can use; no chemistry, no telepathy. It's a way of life; a way of thinking. The aliens have no crime, no misfits. What effort is being made to study their philosophy? Or to set them up as a problem in social engineering?"

Antyok grew thoughtful, and his plump face smoothed out, "It is an interesting consideration. It would be a matter for psychologists—"

"No good. Most of them are quacks. Psychologists point out problems, but their solutions are fallacious. We need men of Aurelion. Men of The Philosophy—"

"But look here, we can't turn Cepheus 18 into . . . into a metaphysical study."

"Why not? It can be done easily."

"How?"

"Forget your puny test-tube peerings. Allow the aliens to set up a society free of Humans. Give them an untrammeled independence and allow an intermingling of philosophies—"

Antyok's nervous response came, "That can't be done in a day."

"We can start in a day."

The administrator said slowly, "Well, I can't prevent you from trying to start." He grew confidential, his mild eyes thoughtful, "You'll ruin your own game, though, if you publish SciGroup 10's report and denounce it on humanitarian grounds. The Scientists are powerful."

"And we of The Philosophy as well."

"Yes, but there's an easy way. You needn't rave. Simply point out that the SciGroup is not solving its problems. Do so unemotionally and let the readers think out your point of view for themselves. Take the birth-rate problem, for instance. *There's* something for you. In a generation, the non-Humans might die out, for all science can do. Point out that a more philosophical approach is required. Or pick some other obvious point. Use your judgment, eh?"

Antyok smiled ingratiatingly as he rose, "But, for the Galaxy's sake, don't stir up a bad smell."

Bannerd was stiff and unresponsive, "You may be right."

It was later that Bannerd wrote in a capsule message to a friend, "He is not clever, by any means. He is confused and has no guiding-line through life. Certainly utterly incompetent in his job. But he's a cutter and a trimmer, compromises his way around difficulties, and will yield concessions rather than risk a hard stand. He may prove valuable in that. Yours in Aurelion."

From: AdHQ-Ceph18
To: BuOuProv
Subject: Birth rate of non-Humans on Cepheus 18, News Report on.
References:
    (a) AdHQ-Ceph18 letr. AA/LA/mn, dated 174/977 G.E.
    (b) Imperial Directive, Ja2374, dated 243/975 G.E.
Enclosures:
    1-G. Bannerd news report, date-lined Cepheus 18, 201/977 G.E.
    2-G Bannerd news report, datelined Cepheus 18, 203/977 G.E.

1. The sterility of non-Humans on Cepheus 18, reported to the BuOuProv in reference (a), has become the subject of news reports to the galactic press. The news reports in question are submitted herewith for the information of the BuOuProv as Enclosures 1 and 2. Although said reports are based on material considered confidential and closed to the public, the news reporter in question maintained his rights to free expression under the terms of reference (b).

2. In view of the unavoidable publicity and misunderstanding on the part of the general public now inevitable, it is requested that the BuOuProv direct future policy on the problem of non-Human sterility.

L. Antyok, Superv, AdHQ-Ceph 18,
209/977 G.E.

From: BuOuProv
To: AdHQ-Ceph 18
Subject: Birth rate of non-Humans on Cepheus 18, Investigation of.
References

(a) AdHQ-Ceph 18 letr. AA-LA/mn, dated 209/977 G.E.

(b) AdHQ-Ceph 18 letr. AA-LA/mn 174/977 G.E.

1. It is proposed to investigate the causes and the means of precluding the unfavorable birth-rate phenomena mentioned in references (a) and (b). A project is therefore set up, entitled, "Birth rate of non-Humans on Cepheus 18, Investigation of" to which, in view of the crucial importance of the subject, a priority of AA is given.

2. The number assigned to the subject project is 2910, and all expenses incidental to it shall be assigned to Appropriation number 18/78.

C. Morily, Chief, BuOuProv,
223/977 G.E.

III.

If Tomor Zammo's ill-humor lessened within the grounds of SciGroup 10 Experimental Station, his friendliness had not thereby increased. Antyok found himself standing alone at the viewing windows into the main field laboratory.

The main field laboratory was a broad court at the environmental conditions of Cepheus 18 itself for the discomfort of the experimenters and the convenience of the experimentees. Through the burning sand, and the dry, oxygen-rich air, there sparkled the hard brilliance of hot, white sunlight. And under the blaze, the brick-red non-Humans, wrinkled of skin and wiry of build, huddled in their squatting positions of ease, by ones and twos.

Zammo emerged from the laboratory. He paused to drink water thirstily. He looked up, moisture gleaming on his upper lip, "Like to step in there?"

Antyok shook his head definitely, "No, thank you. What's the temperature right now?"

"A hundred twenty, if there were shade. And they complain of the cold. It's drinking time now. Want to watch them drink?"

A spray of water shot upward from the fountain in the center of the court, and the little alien figures swayed to their feet and hopped eagerly forward in a queer, springy half-run. They milled about the water, jostling one another. The centers of their faces were suddenly disfigured by the projection of a long and flexible fleshy tube, which thrust forward into the spray and was withdrawn dripping.

It continued for long minutes. The bodies swelled and the wrinkles disappeared. They retreated slowly, backing away, with the drinking tube flicking in and out, before receding finally into a pink, wrinkled mass above a wide, lipless mouth. They went to sleep in groups in the shaded angles, plump and sated.

"Animals!" said Zammo, with contempt.

"How often do they drink?" asked Antyok.

"As often as they want. They can go a week if they have to. We water them every day. They store it under their skin. They eat in the evenings. Vegetarians, you know."

Antyok smiled chubbily, "It's nice to get a bit of firsthand information occasionally. Can't read reports all the time."

"Yes?"—noncommittally. Then, "What's new? What about the lacypants boys on Trantor?"

Antyok shrugged dubiously, "You can't get the Bureau to commit itself, unfortunately. With the Emperor sympathetic to the Aurelionists, humanitarianism is the order of the day. You know that."

There was a pause in which the administrator chewed his lip uncertainly. "But there's this birth-rate problem now. It's finally been assigned to AdHQ, you know—and double A priority, too."

Zammo muttered wordlessly.

Antyok said, "You may not realize it, but that project will now take precedence over all other work proceeding on Cepheus 18. It's important."

He turned back to the viewing window and said thoughtfully with a bald lack of preamble, "Do you think those creatures might be unhappy?"

"Unhappy!" The word was an explosion.

"Well, then," Antyok corrected hastily, "maladjusted. You understand? It's difficult to adjust an environment to a race we know so little of."

"Say—did you ever see the world we took them from?"

"I've read the reports—"

"Reports!"—infinite contempt. "I've *seen* it. This may look like desert out there to you, but it's a watery paradise to those devils. They have all the food and water they can get. They have a world to themselves with vegetation and natural water flow, instead of a lump of silica and granite where fungi were force-grown in caves and water had to be steamed out of gypsum rock. In ten years, they would have been dead to the last beast, and we saved them. Unhappy? Ga-a-ah, if they are, they haven't the decency of most animals."

"Well, perhaps. Yet I have a notion."

"A notion? What is your notion?" Zammo reached for one of his cigars.

"It's something that might help you. Why not study the creatures in a more integrated fashion? Let them use their initiative. After all, they did have a highly-developed science. Your reports speak of it continually. Give them problems to solve."

"Such as?"

"Oh . . . oh," Antyok waved his hands helplessly. "Whatever you think might help most. For instance, space-ships. Get them into the control room and study their reactions."

"Why?" asked Zammo with dry bluntness.

"Because the reaction of their minds to tools and controls adjusted to the human temperament can teach you a lot. In addition, it will make a more effective bribe, it seems to me, than anything you've yet tried. You'll get more volunteers if they think they'll be doing something interesting."

"That's your psychology coming out. Hm-m-m. Sounds better than it probably is. I'll sleep on it. And where would I get permission, in any case, to let them handle spaceships? I've none at *my* disposal, and it would take a good deal longer than it was worth to follow down the line of red tape to get one assigned to us."

Antyok pondered, and his forehead creased lightly, "It doesn't *have* to be spaceships. But even so— If you would write up another report and make the suggestion yourself— strongly, you understand—I might figure out some way of tying it up with my birth-rate project. A double-A priority can get practically anything, you know, without questions."

Zammo's interest lacked a bit even of mildness. "Well, maybe. Meanwhile, I've some basal metabolism tests in progress, and it's getting late. I'll think about it. It's got its points."

From: AdHQ-Ceph18
To: BuOuProv
Subject: Outer Province Project 2910, Part I—Birth rate of non-Humans on Cepheus 18, Investigation of.
Reference:
(a) BuOuProv letr. Ceph-N-CM/car, 115097, 223/977 G.E.
Enclosure:
1. SciGroup 10, Physical & Biochemical Division report, Part XV, dated 220/997 G.E.

1. Enclosure 1 is forwarded herewith for the information of the BuOuProv.

2. Special attention is directed to Section V, Paragraph 3 of Enclosure 1 in which it is requested that a spaceship be assigned SciGroup 10 for use in expediting investigations authorized by the BuOuProv. It is considered by AdHQ-Ceph 18 that such investigations may be of material use in aiding work now in progress on the subject project, authorized by reference (a). It is suggested, in view of the high priority placed by the BuOuProv upon the subject project, that immediate consideration be given the SciGroup's request.

L. Antyok, Superv, AdHQ-Ceph 18,
240/977 G.E.

From: BuOuProv
To: AdHQ-Ceph18
Subject: Outer Province Project 2910—Birth rate of non-Humans on Cepheus 18, Investigation of.
Reference:
(a) AdHQ-Ceph 18 letr. AA-LA/mn, dated 240/977 G.E.

1. Training Ship AN-R-2055 is being placed at the

disposal of AdHQ-Ceph 18 for use in investigation of non-Humans on Cepheus 18 with respect to the subject project and other authorized OuProv projects, as requested in Enclosure 1 to reference (a).

2. It is urgently requested that work on the subject be expedited by all available means.

C. Morily, Head, BuOuProv,
251/977 G.E.

IV.

The little, bricky creature must have been more uncomfortable than his bearing would admit to. He was carefully wrapped in a temperature already adjusted to the point where his human companions steamed in their open shirts.

His speech was high-pitched and careful, "I find it damp, but not unbearably so at this low temperature."

Antyok smiled, "It is nice of you to come. I had planned to visit you, but a trial run in your atmosphere out there—" The smile had become rueful.

"It doesn't matter. You other-worldlings have done more for us than ever we were able to do for ourselves. It is an obligation that is but imperfectly returned by the endurance on my part of a trifling discomfort." His speech seemed always indirect, as if he approached his thoughts sidelong, or as if it were against all etiquette to be blunt.

Gustiv Bannerd, seated in an angle of the room, with one long leg crossing the other, scrawled nimbly and said, "You don't mind if I record all this?"

The Cepheid non-Human glanced briefly at the journalist, "I have no objection."

Antyok's apologetics persisted, "This is not a purely social affair, sir. I would not have forced discomfort on you for that. There are important questions to be considered, and you are the leader of your people."

The Cepheid nodded," I am satisfied your purposes are kindly. Please proceed."

The administrator almost wriggled in his difficulty in putting thoughts into words. "It is a subject," he said, "of delicacy, and one I would never bring up if it weren't for the overwhelming importance of the . . . uh . . . question. I am only the spokesman of my government—"

"My people consider the otherworld government a kindly one."

"Well, yes, they are kindly. For that reason, they are disturbed over the fact that your people no longer breed."

Antyok paused, and waited with worry for a reaction that did not come. The Cepheid's face was motionless except for the soft, trembling motion of the wrinkled area that was his deflated drinking tube.

Antyok continued, "It is a question we have hesitated to bring up because of its extremely personal angles. Noninterference is my government's prime aim, and we have done our best to investigate the problem quietly and without disturbing your people. But, frankly, we—"

"Have failed?" finished the Cepheid, at the other's pause.

"Yes. Or at least, we have not discovered a concrete failure to reproduce the exact environment of your original world; with, of course, the necessary modification to make it more livable. Naturally, it is thought there is some chemical shortcoming. And so I ask your voluntary help in the matter. Your people are advanced in the study of your own biochemistry. If you do not choose, or would rather not—"

"No, no, I can help." The Cepheid seemed cheerful about it. The smooth flat planes of his loose-skinned, hairless skull wrinkled in an alien response to an uncertain emotion. "It is not a matter that any of us would have thought would have disturbed you other-worldlings. That it does is but another indication of your well-meaning kindness. This world we find congenial, a paradise in comparison to our old. It lacks in nothing. Conditions such as now prevail belong in our legends of the Golden Age."

"Well—"

"But there is a something; a something you may not understand. We cannot expect different intelligences to think alike."

"I shall try to understand."

The Cepheid's voice had grown soft, its liquid undertones more pronounced, "We were dying on our native world; but we were fighting. Our science, developed through a history older than yours, was losing; but it had not yet lost. Perhaps it was because our science was fundamentally biological, rather than physical as yours is. Your people discovered new forms of energy and reached the stars. Our people discovered new truths of psychology and psychiatry and built a working society free of disease and crime.

"There is no need to question which of the two angles of approach was the more laudable, but there is no uncertainty as to which proved more successful in the end. In our dying world, without the means of life or sources of power, our biological science could but make the dying easier.

"And yet we fought. For centuries past, we had been groping toward the elements of atomic power, and slowly the spark of hope had glimmered that we might break through the two-dimensional limits of our planetary surface and reach the stars. There were no other planets in our system to serve as stepping stones. Nothing but some twenty light-years to the nearest star, without the knowledge of the possibility of the existence of other planetary systems, but rather of the contrary.

"But there is something in all life that insists on striving; even on useless striving. There were only five thousand of us left in the last days. Only five thousand. And our first ship was ready. It was experimental. It would probably have been a failure. But already we had all the principles of propulsion and navigation correctly worked out."

There was a long pause, and the Cepheid's small black eyes seemed glazed in retrospect.

The newspaperman put in suddenly, from his corner, "And then we came?"

"And then you came," the Cepheid agreed simply. "It changed everything. Energy was ours for the asking. A new world, congenial and, indeed, ideal, was ours even without asking. If our problems of society had long been solved by ourselves, our more difficult problems of environment were suddenly solved for us, no less completely."

"Well?" urged Antyok.

"Well—it was somehow not well. For centuries, our ancestors had fought towards the stars, and now the stars suddenly proved to be the property of others. We had fought for life, and it had become a present handed to us by others. There is no longer any reason to fight. There is no longer anything to attain. All the universe is the property of your race."

"This world is yours," said Antyok, gently.

"By sufferance. It is a gift. It is not ours by right."

"You have earned it, in my opinion."

And now the Cepheid's eyes were sharply fixed on the other's countenance, "You mean well, but I doubt that you understand. We have nowhere to go, save this gift of a world. We are in a blind alley. The function of life is striving, and that is taken from us. Life can no longer interest us. We have no offspring—voluntarily. It is our way of removing ourselves from your way."

Absent-mindedly, Antyok had removed that fluoro-globe from the window seat, and spun it on its base. Its gaudy surface reflected light as it spun, and its three-foot-high bulk floated with incongruous grace and lightness in the air.

Antyok said, "Is that your only solution? Sterility?"

"We might escape still," whispered the Cepheid, "but where in the Galaxy is there place for us? It is all yours."

"Yes, there is no place for you nearer than the Magellanic Clouds if you wished independence. The Magellanic Clouds—"

"And you would not let us go of yourselves. You mean kindly, I know."

"Yes, we mean kindly—but we could not let you go."

"It is a mistaken kindness."

"Perhaps, but could you not reconcile yourselves? You have a world."

"It is something past complete explanations. Your mind is different. We could not reconcile ourselves. I believe, administrator, that you have thought of all this before. The concept of the blind alley we find ourselves trapped in is not new to you."

Antyok looked up, startled, and one hand steadied the fluoro-globe, "Can you read my mind?"

"It is just a guess. A good one, I think."

"Yes—but *can* you read my mind? The minds of humans in general, I mean. It is an interesting point. The scientists say you cannot, but sometimes I wonder if it is that you simply will not. Could you answer that? I am detaining you, unduly, perhaps."

"No . . . no—" But the little Cepheid drew his enveloping robe closer, and buried his face in the electrically-heated pad at the collar for a moment. "You other-worldlings speak of reading minds. It is not so at all, but it is assuredly hopeless to explain."

Antyok mumbled the old proverb, "One cannot explain sight to a man blind from birth."

"Yes, just so. This sense which you call 'mind reading,' quite erroneously, cannot be applied to us. It is not that we cannot receive the proper sensations, it is that your people do not transmit them, and we have no way of explaining to you how to go about it."

"Hm-m-m."

"There are times, of course, of great concentration or emotional tension on the part of an other-worldling when some of us who are more expert in this sense; more sharp-eyed, so to speak; detect vaguely *something*. It is uncertain; yet I myself have at times wondered—"

Carefully, Antyok began spinning the fluoro-globe once more. His pink face was set in thought, and his eyes were fixed upon the Cepheid. Gustiv Bannerd stretched his fingers and reread his notes, his lips moving silently.

The fluoro-globe spun, and slowly the Cepheid seemed to grow tense as well, as his eyes shifted to the colorful sheen of the globe's fragile surface.

The Cepheid said, "What is that?"

Antyok started, and his face smoothed into an almost chuckling placidity, "This? A Galactic fad of three years ago; which means that it is a hopelessly old-fashioned relic this year. It is a useless device but it looks pretty. Bannerd, could you adjust the windows to nontransmission?"

There was the soft click of a contact, and the windows became curved regions of darkness, while in the center of the room, the fluoro-globe was suddenly the focus of a rosy effulgence that seemed to leap outward in streamers. Antyok, a scarlet figure in a scarlet room, placed it upon the table and spun it with a hand that dripped red. As it spun, the colors changed with a slowly increasing rapidity, blended and fell apart into more extreme contrasts.

Antyok was speaking in an eerie atmosphere of molten, shifting rainbow, "The surface is of a material that exhibits variable fluorescence. It is almost weightless, extremely fragile, but gyroscopically balanced so that it rarely falls, with ordinary care. It is rather pretty, don't you think?"

From somewhere the Cepheid's voice came, "Extremely pretty."

"But it has outworn its welcome; outlived its fashionable existence."

The Cepheid's voice was abstracted, "It is very pretty."

Bannerd restored the light at a gesture, and the colors faded.

The Cepheid said, "That is something my people would enjoy." He stared at the globe with fascination.

And now Antyok rose. "You had better go. If you stay

longer, the atmosphere may have bad effects. I thank you humbly for your kindness."

"I thank you humbly for yours." The Cepheid had also risen.

Antyok said, "Most of your people, by the way, have accepted our offers to them to study the make-up of our modern spaceships. You understand, I suppose, that the purpose was to study the reactions of your people to our technology. I trust that conforms with your sense of propriety."

"You need not apologize. I, myself, have now the makings of a human pilot. It was most interesting. It recalls our own efforts—and reminds us of how nearly on the right track we were."

The Cepheid left, and Antyok sat, frowning.

"Well," he said to Bannerd, a little sharply. "You remember our agreement, I hope. This interview can't be published."

Bannerd shrugged, "Very well."

Antyok was at his seat, and his fingers fumbled with the small metal figurine upon his desk, "What do you think of all this, Bannerd?"

"I am sorry for them. I think I understand how they feel. We must educate them out of it. The Philosophy can do it."

"You think so?"

"Yes."

"We can't let them go, of course."

"Oh, no. Out of the question. We have too much to learn from them. This feeling of theirs is only a passing stage. They'll think differently, especially when we allow them the completest independence."

"Maybe. What do you think of the fluoro-globes, Bannerd? He liked them. It might be a gesture of the right sort to order several thousand of them. The Galaxy knows, they're a drug on the market right now, and cheap enough."

"Sounds like a good idea," said Bannerd.

"The Bureau would never agree, though. I know them."

The newsman's eyes narrowed, "But it might be just the thing. They need new interests."

"Yes? Well, we *could* do something. I could include your transcript of the interview as part of a report and just emphasize the matter of the globes a bit. After all, you're a member of The Philosophy and might have influence with important people, whose word with the Bureau might carry much more weight than mine. You understand—?"

"Yes," mused Bannerd. "Yes."

From: AdHQ-Ceph18

To: BuOuProv

Subject: OuProv Project 2910, Part II; Birth rate of non-Humans on Cepheus 18, Investigation of.

Reference:

(a) BuOuProv letr. Ceph-N-CM/car, 115097, dated 223/977 G.E.

Enclosure:

1. Transcript of conversation between L. Antyok of AdHQ-Ceph 18, and Ni-San, High Judge of the non-Humans on Cepheus 18.

1. Enclosure 1 is forwarded herewith for the information of the BuOuProv.

2. The investigation of the subject project undertaken in response to the authorization of reference (a) is being pursued along the new lines indicated in Enclosure 1. The BuOuProv is assured that every means will be used to combat the harmful psychological attitude at present prevalent among the non-Humans.

3. It is to be noted that the High Judge of the non-Humans on Cepheus 18 expressed interest in fluoro-globes. A preliminary investigation into this fact of non-Human psychology had been initiated.

L. Antyok, Superv, AdHQ-Ceph 18,
272/977 G.E.

From: BuOuProv
To: AdHQ-Ceph 18
Subject: OuProv Project 2910; Birth rate of non-Humans on Cepheus 18, Investigation of.
Reference:
  (a) AdHQ-Ceph 18 letr. AA-LA/mn, dated 272/977 G.E.
1. With reference to Enclosure 1 of reference (a), five thousand fluoro-globes have been allocated for shipment to Cepheus 18, by the Department of Trade.
2. It is instructed that AdHQ-Ceph 18 make use of all methods of appeasing non-Humans' dissatisfaction, consistent with the necessities of obedience to Imperial proclamations.

C. Morily, Chief, BuOuProv,
283/977 G.E.

V.

The dinner was over, the wine had been brought in, and the cigars were out. The groups of talkers had formed, and the captain of the merchant fleet was the center of the largest. His brilliant white uniform quite outsparkled his listeners.

He was almost complacent in his speech: "The trip was nothing. I've had more than three hundred ships under me before this. Still, I've never had a cargo quite like this. What do you want with five thousand fluoro-globes on this desert, by the Galaxy!"

Loodun Antyok laughed gently. He shrugged, "For the non-Humans. It wasn't a difficult cargo, I hope."

"No, not difficult. But bulky. They're fragile, and I couldn't carry more than twenty to a ship, with all the government regulations concerning packing and precautions against breakage. But it's the government's money, I suppose."

Zammo smiled grimly. "Is this your first experience with government methods, captain?"

"Galaxy, no," exploded the spaceman. "I try to avoid it, of course, but you can't help getting entangled on occasion. And it's an abhorrent thing when you are, and that's the truth. The red tape! The paper work! It's enough to stunt your growth and curdle your circulation. It's a tumor, a cancerous growth on the Galaxy. I'd wipe out the whole mess."

Antyok said, "You're unfair, captain. You don't understand."

"Yes? Well, now, as one of these bureaucrats," and he smiled amiably at the word, "suppose you explain your side of the situation, administrator."

"Well, now," Antyok seemed confused, "government is a serious and complicated business. We've got thousands of planets to worry about in this Empire of ours and billions of people. It's almost past human ability to supervise the business of governing without the tightest sort of organization. I think there are something like four hundred million men today in the Imperial Administrative Service alone, and in order to co-ordinate their efforts and to pool their knowledge, you *must* have what you call red tape and paper work. Every bit of it, senseless though it may seem, annoying though it may be, has its uses. Every piece of paper is a thread binding the labors of four hundred million humans. Abolish the Administrative Service and you abolish the Empire; and with it, interstellar peace, order, and civilization."

"Come—" said the captain.

"No. I mean it." Antyok was earnestly breathless. "The rules and system of the Administrative set-up must be sufficiently all-embracing and rigid so that in case of incompetent officials, and sometimes one *is* appointed— you may laugh, but there are incompetent scientists, and newsmen, and captains, too—in case of incompetent officials, I say, little harm will be done. For, at the worst, the system can move by itself."

"Yes," grunted the captain, sourly, "and if a capable administrator should be appointed? He is then caught by the same rigid web and is forced into mediocrity."

"Not at all," replied Antyok, warmly. "A capable man can work within the limits of the rules and accomplish what he wishes."

"How?" asked Bannerd.

"Well . . . well—" Antyok was suddenly ill at ease. "One method is to get yourself an A-priority project, or double-A, if possible."

The captain leaned his head back for laughter, but never quite made it, for the door was flung open and frightened men were pouring in. The shouts made no sense at first. Then:

"Sir, the ships are gone. These non-Humans have taken them by force."

"What? All?"

"Every one. Ships and creatures—"

It was two hours later that the four were together again, alone in Antyok's office now.

Antyok said coldly, "They've made no mistakes. There's not a ship left behind, not even your training ship, Zammo. And there isn't a government ship available in this entire half of the Sector. By the time we organize a pursuit they'll be out of the Galaxy and halfway to the Magellanic Clouds. Captain, it was your responsibility to maintain an adequate guard."

The captain cried, "It was our first day out of space. Who could have known—"

Zammo interrupted fiercely, "Wait a while, captain. I'm beginning to understand. Antyok," his voice was hard, "you engineered this."

"I?" Antyok's expression was strangely cool, almost indifferent.

"You told us this evening that a clever administrator got an A-priority project assigned to accomplish what he wished. You got such a project in order to help the non-Humans escape."

"I did? I beg your pardon, but how could that be? It was you yourself in one of your reports that brought up the problem of the failing birth rate. It was Bannerd, here, whose sensational articles frightened the Bureau into making a double A-priority project out of it. I had nothing to do with it."

"*You* suggested that I mention the birth rate," said Zammo, violently.

"Did I?" said Antyok, composedly.

"And for that matter," roared Bannerd, suddenly, "you suggested that I mention the birth rate in my articles."

The three ringed him now and hemmed him in. Antyok leaned back in his chair and said easily, "I don't know what you mean by suggestions. If you are accusing me, please stick to evidence—legal evidence. The laws of the Empire go by written, filmed, or transcribed material, or by witnessed statements. All my letters as administrator are on file here, at the Bureau, and at other places. I never asked for an A-priority project. The Bureau assigned it to me, and Zammo and Bannerd are responsible for that. In print, at any rate."

Zammo's voice was an almost inarticulate growl, "You hoodwinked me into teaching the creatures how to handle a spaceship."

"It was *your* suggestion. I have your report proposing they be studied in their reaction to human tools on file. So has the Bureau. The evidence—the *legal* evidence, is plain. I had nothing to do with it."

"Nor with the globes?" demanded Bannerd.

The captain howled suddenly, "You had my ships brought here purposely. Five thousand globes! You knew it would require hundreds of craft."

"I never asked for globes," said Antyok, coldly. "That was the Bureau's idea, although I think Bannerd's friends of The Philosophy helped that along."

Bannerd fairly choked. He spat out, "You were asking that Cepheid leader if he could read minds. You were telling him to express interest in the globes."

"Come, now. You prepared the transcript of the conversation yourself, and that, too, is on file. You can't prove it." He stood up. "You'll have to excuse me. I must prepare a report for the Bureau."

At the door, Antyok turned. "In a way, the problem of the non-Humans is solved, even if only to their own satisfaction. They'll breed now, and have a world they've earned themselves. It's what they wanted.

"Another thing. Don't accuse me of silly things. I've been in the Service for twenty-seven years, and I assure you that my paper work is proof enough that I have been thoroughly correct in everything I have done. And captain, I'll be glad to continue our discussion of earlier this evening at your convenience and explain how a capable administrator can work through red tape and still get what he wants."

It was remarkable that such a round, smooth baby-face could wear a smile quite so sardonic.

From: BuOuProv
To: Loodun Antyok, Chief Public Administrator, A-8
Subject: Administrative Service, Standing in.
Reference:
   (a) AdServ Court Decision 22874-Q, dated 1/978 G.E.
1. In view of the favorable opinion handed down in reference (a) you are hereby absolved of all responsibility for the flight of non-Humans on Cepheus 18. It is requested that you hold yourself in readiness for your next appointment.

R. Horpritt, Chief, AdServ,
15/978 G.E.